A Candlelight Ecstasy Romance®

"WHY ARE YOU UNDRESSING ME?" RUTH CRIED.

"Oh, stop complaining. I just dragged you out of a freezing lake, and now I've got to get these clothes off you before you turn into a blond icicle."

"A few days ago you couldn't stand the sight of me, and now you're ripping my clothes off!"

Then she caught sight of Frank's naked chest and swallowed hard. She was still trembling, but not just from the cold.

Suddenly she realized that he was right; he *had* saved her life. Contritely she began, "I might have been too hasty—"

But he wasn't about to listen. "Stuff it," he said wearily, and while her mouth was still open in a gasp of astonishment, he hefted her over his bare shoulder and carried her off.

CANDLELIGHT ECSTASY CLASSIC ROMANCES . . .

WAGERED WEEKEND,
Jayne Castle

LOVE'S ENCORE,
Rachel Ryan

SURRENDER BY MOONLIGHT,
Bonnie Drake

THE FACE OF LOVE,
Anne Reisser

CANDLELIGHT ECSTASY ROMANCES®

QUANTITY SALES

INDIVIDUAL SALES

WORTH HIS WEIGHT IN GOLD

Molly Katz

A CANDLELIGHT ECSTASY ROMANCE®

Published by
Dell Publishing Co., Inc.
1 Dag Hammarskjold Plaza
New York, New York 10017

Dell ® TM 681510, Dell Publishing Co., Inc.

Candlelight Ecstasy Romance®, 1,203,540, is a registered
trademark of Dell Publishing Co., Inc., New York, New York.

ISBN: 0–440–19792–9

Printed in the United States of America

January 1987

10 9 8 7 6 5 4 3 2 1

WFH

Dedicated to my late father and my mother,
Hubert and Betty Chuckrow Simon

Thanks to Chief Kevin Costello, Dobbs Ferry,
N.Y., Police Department, for his cheerful
patience

To Our Readers:

We have been delighted with your enthusiastic response to Candlelight Ecstasy Romances®, and we thank you for the interest you have shown in this exciting series.

In the upcoming months we will continue to present the distinctive sensuous love stories you have come to expect only from Ecstasy. We look forward to bringing you many more books from your favorite authors and also the very finest work from new authors of contemporary romantic fiction.

As always, we are striving to present the unique, absorbing love stories that you enjoy most—books that are more than ordinary romance. Your suggestions and comments are always welcome. Please write to us at the address below.

Sincerely,

The Editors
Candlelight Romances
1 Dag Hammarskjold Plaza
New York, New York 10017

WORTH HIS WEIGHT IN GOLD

"Mayor on Line Two, Chief."

"Thanks. Hello, Norman? What's up?"

"I'll come right to the point, Frank. We've had two muggings this month—"

"I know we have, Norman. I can count."

"Well, people are asking me what the police are doing. What do I tell them?"

"Tell them the truth. We've got a lot of teenaged delinquents out there, and we're doing our best to protect the folks."

"But *are* you?"

"What the hell are you talking about, Norman?"

"Bennett's article in the *Banner,* where the health expert he interviewed says you guys are too fat to catch these teenagers. People are angry. They see more crime, they see their police department overweight, they want action. I'll ask you again, Frank. What do I tell them?"

"Tell them to leave police business to the police."

"Chief! Chief Gordon! Glad I bumped into you."

"I'm in a hurry, Mr. Mosely. Can it wait?"

"It shouldn't, Chief. Seems like it's waited too long already, if you get my drift."

"I don't—"

"As chamber of commerce president, I've been asked to tell you that the members want to see changes in the department. Changes in your weight, to be exact."

"Don't believe everything you read in the paper, Mr. Mosely. The department happens to be doing an excellent job. If you and the chamber of commerce don't like it, then you and the chamber of commerce can move to Moscow. I expect the police are pretty thin there."

"Chief, wait! Chief—"

"Hello, Chief Gordon? John Bennett. I'm with the *Banner*. I wrote the piece about—"

"Yeah, I know who you are, Bennett. What the hell do you want now?"

"I'm planning a follow-up article, and I'd like to interview you about your plans for getting the department into better shape."

"My *plans* are to get my hands on the 'health expert' who started all this."

"What, Chief? I can't hear you. *How* will you get the department in shape?"

"*Can you hear me now, Bennett?* The department is in shape to do what it has to. We're fine officers; we do an excellent job. How cute the men look is irrelevant. That's all I have to say."

"But—"

"I said that's *it!* Get off my case!"

He slammed down the phone.

CHAPTER ONE

Ruth couldn't believe her eyes when the old man raised the rifle. She halted, her thick soles skidding a little in the sand on the road, and stood there breathing harshly, her heart pounding. She hadn't seen a .22 since she used to fire them on a range in high school, and she hadn't ever seen one from this angle. The barrel was leveled right at her nose.

"Warned ya," he said, squinting behind the gun butt. He wore seersucker pants that hung on his skinny frame, a flannel shirt, and a sleeveless down vest. A mop of unhealthy-looking gray hair sat atop a wrinkled, hostile face that hadn't been shaved in a week or so. "Thought I was just foolin', ain't that right?"

Ruth swallowed. "I believe you. Could you put that down? I'll just go back along the road and—"

"No, ma'am!" he roared. "You come with me." He lowered the rifle and gestured with it for her to follow him into his house.

"What? In *there?* I will not!"

Slowly the old man lifted the gun again.

"Stop that," Ruth said. "You can't point a rifle at people for no reason. I haven't done anything." Her heart was threatening to leap through her ribs.

"Man can defend his property against trespassers. You get inside while I call the police. I'm not riskin' you runnin' off."

The police. Thank heaven. They'd tell this maniac he couldn't wave a gun around. She'd just have to hold back her panic and be careful not to provoke the man further until they came.

He backed slowly into the house, keeping his eyes on her and the rifle at a ready angle. Ruth followed.

She'd known something was up the minute she reached the top of the hill and saw Mr. Zachariah already outside waiting for her, his hands behind him. Usually he came charging out after she'd passed, yelling at her disappearing back. She was fast enough to cover a good chunk of ground before he could mobilize his eighty-year-old reflexes to get out the door and into the yard, so she never heard much of what he yelled—but she didn't have to. She knew what was bothering him.

For some reason Mr. Zachariah considered his property, including the road she liked to run on, to be sacred ground he didn't want violated even by a pair of size seven ladies' sneakers. But his road was the only uphill route to the lake track where she did most of her run, and she badly needed that initial workout. So she just tried to close her ears to his ranting.

Everybody in town knew Mr. Zachariah was a troublemaker. It wasn't only trespassers who got his abuse; he was always screaming at the kids in her building for various imaginary sins, even when they were nowhere near his property.

But Ruth's defiance seemed to inflame him more than anything. He was out there every day, cursing her. She hated it, but not as much as she hated the

14

threat of losing her beloved route. She'd figured that if she ignored him long enough, he'd find some more rewarding target for his rage and give up on her.

Obviously, she'd figured wrong.

He locked and bolted the door behind her. He went to a table that held an old black phone and dialed with a bony finger, glancing Ruth's way after each digit. When she lifted her hand to wipe sweat from her face, he raised the rifle to her nose again. She clasped her hands in front of her and clenched them hard.

The old man spoke into the phone, covering his mouth.

"Be here right away," he told Ruth. "You can just stay put."

And she did, keeping her feet where they were, afraid to move an inch. She longed to wipe her damp hands on her sweat pants, brush her hair back off her face, break her tension with some movement, but she didn't dare. Who knew what this psychopath might take it into his head to do?

She looked around, desperate for something to focus on besides the angry old man and his gun. The house had a closed-up smell, as though no outside air ever came in. There wasn't much furniture.

She tried to concentrate on the hardwood floor. Vaguely, through her fear, she knew it had a nice dark stain that would look good in the ten-unit building she owned. She made herself picture some of the kids helping her do the sanding.

But it was no use; she wasn't succeeding at distracting herself. Her clasped hands had begun to shake. She needed something else to look at. Mr. Zachariah had lowered the rifle from her face, but it wasn't much more comforting to have it directed at her stomach.

She was sweating more, in spite of the cold house, and she was afraid she might start to cry.

There was a staircase to her left. She made herself examine it, concentrating. It was a rickety thing that didn't look as if it could support the weight of a spider.

She glanced at Mr. Zachariah, and back at the stairs. They really *didn't* look as though they could hold him. He was thin, but he wasn't invisible.

The sun must have gone behind a cloud because the house grew darker, and Ruth felt fear spreading up her neck.

The staircase. I'll keep thinking about the staircase.

Maybe there was another way to get up and down— back steps or something. Or a fireman's pole. She pictured Mr. Zachariah, his stubbled jowls peeking out beneath a fire hat, shimmying down a pole, and in spite of the ice in her stomach she smiled.

"Somethin' funny?" the man demanded, his hands tightening on the rifle.

"No," she said, startled. She had to watch herself. The old lunatic would be delighted with any excuse to pull the trigger.

Just then Ruth heard a car come to a stop. The engine died and a door slammed. She let out her breath and had to hold on to a door molding to keep herself from sinking to the floor in relief.

With a final venomous glance at her, the old man went to the door and unlocked it.

An extremely large policeman in sunglasses came in, ducking slightly under the doorway.

"He has a gun," Ruth said quickly.

"I can see that, thank you. You were trespassing?"

"I . . ." She stopped. It wasn't what she'd expected to hear.

16

"Well?" the policeman demanded.

She took a deep breath and told herself to calm down. It was okay now.

"I was running past here," she began, her voice trembling a little, "when this lunatic pointed a rifle at my—"

"This is a private road. You can't run on it if Mr. Zachariah doesn't want you to."

"But he threatened me! He's always been verbally abusive, and now he's forced me into his house at gunpoint!"

The policeman turned to the old man, who shrugged and looked not at all penitent. "Had to keep her here. She'd'a took off."

"Put the rifle away," the policeman said.

"But—"

"Get it *out* of here. You don't have the right to use a gun to defend your property against a trespasser. There was no threat of danger to you." He nodded toward Ruth. "I'll make sure you have no more trouble with this woman." He turned to the door.

"Wait a minute," Ruth cried, her eyes filling with tears of frustration. "Is that all you're going to do?"

His eyes narrowed. "That's all I'm going to do to Mr. Zachariah," he said meaningfully.

"But he—this is a crime. Isn't it?"

"What crime? Did he hurt you?" the policeman asked.

"No, not exactly, but—"

"Then you've got nothing to squawk about."

"You can't be serious. He terrorized me!" It was becoming clear that this enormous, implacable lion of a man was monumentally uninterested in what she had to say. "How can he get away with that when I haven't done anything wrong? It's unbelievable!"

"I'll be going, Mr. Zachariah," he said, moving to the door. "You stash that rifle, now."

"If you say so, Chief."

"Oh, the heck with it," Ruth said, brushing past him. She hadn't recognized the policeman as the chief. He probably knew who she was. She wouldn't have thought that would matter if her life was in danger, but apparently she was wrong.

She yanked open the door. "The next time I need real protection, I'll know where not to look," she said.

A hand gripped her upper arm. "Slow down, lady. I have a few things to say to you."

"I don't want to hear them. Let go of me!"

"Not a chance." He loosened his hold, but steered her down the walk and out to the road where the cruiser was parked. He let go then, as if dropping a loathsome object. The February wind lifted his longish wavy sandy-brown hair, and he stuck his bare hands in the pockets of the leather jacket he wore over his uniform.

Ruth said, "Tell me something. Are you always this rude to victims? How do you treat people who've been robbed? Beat them up?"

"Listen to me," he said, "because I'm only going to explain this once. And keep your cracks to yourself, starting now." He leaned his massive body back against the car and planted his feet apart. "You can't run on this road. You know damn well there are two other ways to reach the track from Crestview— through Geary Street, or down the hill off the Lake Road. You don't need to get to it through here."

"But I do! It's the only uphill grade within—"

18

"I said you don't! Hear me?"

Ruth took an unthinking step back from the thunderous volume of his voice and stumbled on a stone. The chief grabbed her shoulder to steady her, and got a handful of her blond hair.

"Ouch!" she cried, shaking free. "I told you before, keep your stupid hands off me."

"Lady," he said, "you're really ticking me off. I should have let you fall. For that matter, I should have arranged it."

She looked at him. "Then you do know who I am."

"Finally figured that out, did you? And you call *me* stupid. You're damn right I know who you are. I've been planning to have a little . . . *talk* with you. When I heard Zachariah had caught a trespasser named Barrett running on his road, I decided to come myself. I don't usually go on calls." He took off his sunglasses and put them in a jacket pocket.

So he'd been waiting for an opportunity to get her. She'd walked—run—into a trap. A frightening, infuriating trap. She wiped her face but stayed where she was, her clear blue-gray eyes not wavering from his brown ones.

"You're sweating," he said.

"Well, *you,*" Ruth shot back, "don't sweat enough. Look, you oversize cowboy, you can try all you want to intimidate me, but it won't work. I'm not sorry I said those things in that interview. You deserve them. Half the force needs to lose weight." Her courage wasn't all real—she couldn't help but feel uneasy with this giant looming over her in his menacing way—but she'd be damned if she'd dissolve just because he thought he could make her by yelling and stomping around.

" 'Shockingly pudgy,' " he mimicked cruelly.

19

"Where do you get your gall? What the hell business is it of yours to go telling reporters how I should run my department?"

"I didn't exactly call a press conference. You make it sound as though I was quoted in *Newsweek.* All I did was tell the *Banner,* when they interviewed me after I won the 10K race, that I think several men on the force are too fat—and fat men can't expect to catch muggers. That's why so many of them get away!"

" 'Pillsbury Doughboy,' wasn't it? 'Even the chief himself looks like the Pillsbury Doughboy.' When the hell have you ever met me? Seen me?"

"I've seen your picture."

"Great, lady. Nice going."

"My name," she bit out, "is Ruth."

"Ruth*less* is more like it. Are you so ignorant, Ruthless, that you don't even know a camera adds weight?" He struck a pose, muscles flexed, hips jutting forward. "Do I look like the damn Pillsbury Doughboy to you now?"

"I can't tell with you in that jacket," she said defiantly.

"I'll take it off, then!" he yelled, going for the zipper.

"Don't bother!" she yelled back, and the flutter she'd felt inside at the idea of his taking his clothes off, at the way the contours of his lower body showed against his pants before he dropped the pose, made her continue even more harshly, "You don't have anything I'm interested in looking at!"

"You don't have to be interested, cookie. You've just got to look long enough so you can make a phone call —to the *Banner,* to explain that you were a little hasty and out of line."

20

"But I wasn't either of those things, and you know it. I told the truth. Your department has a problem."

The chief slammed the cruiser's hood with the flat of his hand. "If *I* say the department doesn't have a problem, then it doesn't, do you understand? There's only one problem the department has right now, and it's you, lady, you and your damn big mouth. Do you have any idea what a firestorm you stuck me with?"

"I—"

"The whole town's on my back. I get phone calls, I get letters, I can't walk down the street without somebody buttonholing me to ask how come my men aren't *fit.*" He spat the word.

"You can't blame me—" she began.

"Hell, yes, I blame you. Nobody *but* you! Dumb as it is, people think you're a damn expert. You run in races all over the area, you teach at that exercise place—you even have a college degree in hopscotch or something, don't you?"

"Physical education," Ruth corrected tightly.

"Yeah. Like I said, hopscotch." He hit his left palm with his right fist. "Well, people pay attention to that garbage. Now they have something to blame the muggings on, courtesy of Ruth Barrett, *expert.*"

"But the muggings *are* way up!" Ruth said. "Of course the shape your men are in affects that. You should all trim down."

The chief snorted. "We're supposed to be doing police work, not training for a damn marathon. I do *not* have time to waste on this public relations bull."

When he'd unzipped his jacket it hadn't opened fully, but now it did, falling away from his middle. Ruth could see why he thought he had a valid argument; the extra fifteen pounds or so he carried didn't

21

add much bulk on a man so hugely tall and well muscled. She had to acknowledge that his excellent build was hardly affected by the added weight, at least to the casual eye. But regardless, she told herself, fifteen pounds made him that much less agile, and as for the other men . . . well, the four who really needed to lose could stand to drop nearly two hundred pounds between them.

"By the way," the chief said with a nasty grin, "we have the *Banner* article posted over at the station. You ought to come and see it. It's picked up some additions."

"Additions?" she asked, trying not to look at the holstered revolver that hung at his right hip.

"That's right. A few hunks of gum, some burn holes, coffee—who knows what else."

"You probably wish you could do that to me instead of the clipping," she said, her voice flat with anger. He didn't respond for a long moment, and his silence—as well as the bitter resentment she saw in his eyes—chilled her.

Finally he answered, "Let's just say you're not one of my favorite people. Are you going to make that phone call?"

Ruth folded her arms. "What do you think?"

The chief folded his. "I think I should leave you here with the old man and his gun."

She swallowed. "You'd do that, wouldn't you?"

"Don't test me."

"Believe me, I won't," she said. "I can see you're capable of anything. You find an innocent person being threatened with a deadly weapon, and you think a scolding is all that's necessary."

"You weren't being threatened with a deadly weapon."

"The hell I wasn't!" Ruth shouted. "Mr. Zachariah had that gun pointed right at me. He was just panting—"

"It wasn't loaded."

"—for an excuse to fire it. If I hadn't had the sense to stand still and not—"

"I said it wasn't *loaded,* you dope!"

Ruth's mouth dropped open. "What?"

"You heard me. He said when he called in that he was holding an unloaded weapon."

Ruth stared at him unbelievingly. "So that whole thing was a charade? I was terrified for nothing—and you don't even *tell* me until now? How could you do that?"

"I've never done anything like it before. But as I mentioned," he said, the cruel grin back in place, "you're not one of my favorite people."

"You miserable, bullying—"

"Don't bother, honey. Sticks and stones. Just keep your mouth shut from now on. And stay away from this property."

"You're serious?" She reached up to wipe her face again, but decided not to give him the satisfaction of knowing that he was still making her sweat. She pushed her hair back instead. "I really can't run up here? You won't say anything to that horrible old man?"

His eyes nailed hers. "You'll be lucky if I don't buy him some bullets."

"You're disgusting."

"No I'm not. Not yet. Try pushing me some more."

"Look," she said, "you don't understand what this

23

means to a runner. I need the uphill part of the course. What am I supposed to do for the extra workout?"

"You can do cartwheels on the damn interstate for all I care." He opened the car door and got in. The motor started with a blast of noise. "I told you I was only going to say it once. You'd better pay attention. Don't let me catch you here again."

Wanting to scream out her frustration and fury, Ruth did what she frequently did instead. She raced off, her soles slapping the pavement, knowing she shouldn't start so fast without stretching again yet not caring.

The chief watched her go. He'd known the witch would do that, give him one last zap by continuing on this course instead of going back to her street and using one of the routes he'd told her to. Well, let her; it would be the last time. Even she wasn't enough of a fool to take the risk after he'd outlined the facts for her.

She was out of his sight fast, but not before he'd gotten much more of an eyeful than he would have expected. Up close she wasn't bad-looking, he couldn't help noticing that. But from here, watching her run off, the view was startlingly lovely. Her thick, glossy blond hair streaming out behind her . . . long legs flying high as she sprinted . . . the prettiest, roundest behind he'd seen in a month of Tuesdays. Even the bulky sweat suit couldn't hide her lithe, streamlined form. If he hadn't known she was over thirty, he wouldn't have believed it. She looked like a kid.

For a moment, but only a moment, he felt too old and too slow, the personification of all she'd called him. Then his anger rose again—the fury that had

24

been simmering for two weeks, ever since she had shot her mouth off in the Lakeboro *Banner*. What he'd told her was no exaggeration. She'd caused him more trouble than he'd ever had as chief. The department's image was really suffering. What a crock—as if his men were actually standing around huffing and puffing while the delinquents took over the Lakes Region.

He released the handbrake and shifted. He turned in the old man's driveway and went down the hill to go back to the station. He took his sunglasses out of his pocket, used them to scratch his nose, and put them on the dash; but immediately he brought his hand back to his face. What was that smell?

Passing her building on Crestview did it, jogged his mind somehow so that the answer was right there. Her scent. Her damn perfume. It was a strong, sensuous fragrance, not at all the kind you'd think an athlete would use; he'd have figured she'd smell like witch hazel. But there it was, on the cuff of his leather jacket, noticeable enough so that, unless he took the thing off and stashed it before he ran into any of the men, there'd be one more thing to tease him about.

He groaned and headed into town.

Ruth felt stinging little stabs in her lungs and knew she'd better cool down before she went in. She slowed to a jog and loped all the way down Crestview and back, letting her limbs and muscles loosen. She was damp all over, sweaty despite the frigid wind, but she'd needed to work off her fury at the police chief, that sandy-haired storm trooper, and what was left of her fear from the Zachariah Standoff.

She spent another five minutes walking and then went around her building to the back door, so the sand that always got packed into her shoe treads wouldn't leave a trail in the little lobby. Another nice thing about spring coming—they'd stop sanding the roads. Of course, it was vital in winter, but if you did most of your mileage on shoes instead of tires, a sandy surface was nearly as slippery as an icy one, and the remnants made a mess.

Some of the kids were shooting baskets in the parking lot. She smiled and waved. A tall redhead broke away from the group and came over to Ruth.

"Good run?" he asked. "You look like you had a workout."

She chuckled without humor. "You can say that again."

"You look like you—"

"Okay." She laughed, for real this time, and reached for the door. "I'll see you."

"Ruth, um, wait. Can I talk to you?"

"Sure," she said. "What is it?"

"It's Bridget. I don't think she likes me anymore."

Whatever Ruth was going to say went out of her head then. One of the other boys brushed past them, and the sight of wide shoulders in a leather jacket brought a picture crashing back. She remembered the police chief looking down at her, the feel of his huge hand on her, tangled in her hair, catching her before she could fall—and the way, earlier, he'd held her arm as they left the house. Both times she'd irately shaken him off, jumping away as though his hand had stung her through her sweatshirt—as though she couldn't stand the contact even for an instant. But she'd done that to cover her real reaction: the odd little tremor of pleasure that, in spite of her rage, was spreading through her body at his touch.

26

"Ruth?" Mike said, peering at her. "Are you okay?"

"More or less."

"Can I tell you about Bridget?"

Frank Gordon. That was his name. She'd just thought of it.

"Ruth?"

"Uh, yes, Mike," she said. "I'm sorry. What's the problem?"

"Well, I'm not as heavy with her as she is with me. I mean, I don't think I'm very important to her. Maybe you could give me some, like, tips on what to do."

Ruth refrained from pointing out that, on the basis of her experiences today, she was as good an example of interpersonal relations as the Ayatollah Khomeini.

She leaned against the white clapboard wall of the building, wrapping her arms around herself to fight the chill that was setting in.

"How do you want things to be different?" she asked.

"I kind of wish she had more time for me. Like today. She's supposed to come over so we can do homework together, right? But she had to call her girlfriend. I said why couldn't she call from here, and she said I didn't understand."

"Mike!" one of the boys shouted. "You coming? We're starting a game."

"In a second." He turned back to Ruth. "When I go to her house, I can't wait to get there right after school."

"It's not the same thing."

"Aw. That's what Bridget says."

"But it's not, Mike. It has nothing to do with you." He stared. "She says that too."

"Well, I don't have X-ray ears," Ruth said. "I just

know girls. And the thing is, they have to talk to each other. They *need* to."

"But why? What's so important?"

"Everything. Anything. Girls tell other girls things they don't tell anyone else. They tell them things they don't tell *themselves*. You just have to try and understand."

"I don't."

"I know. Men never do."

"Mike! Can we start, or what?"

"I gotta go. But thanks. This stuff is a pain. I can't wait till I'm older." He ran back to the hoop.

Ruth dashed upstairs to her warm apartment. If her blood weren't approaching a standstill in her veins, she'd be laughing.

Mike was in for a shock if he thought the intricacies between men and women got simpler as they got older. What had happened to her this afternoon was a prime example of how simple they weren't. She shuddered every time she thought of that rude, tyrannical Frank Gordon, how he'd cooperated in Mr. Zachariah's masquerade that had scared her nearly to tears, and what a bullheaded jerk he was about the fitness issue—especially since, despite all this, there was something about the man that made her feel very warm and funny inside. And if that wasn't a "pain," as Mike put it, she didn't know what was!

CHAPTER TWO

Ruth zipped her duffel bag shut and went out to the fitness center's parking lot. It had snowed a little during the afternoon, and a powdery film covered the cars.

She put her bag in the back of her Toyota and drove slowly out to Route 3, nudging the brake to see how slippery the road was. Satisfied that there was no problem, she sped up to forty and headed for the supermarket. It was too sloppy for running, but there was enough time and daylight for a good long walk before her neighbor and good friend Joan Lindsay came for dinner, if she shopped fast.

The lot was crowded, so she pulled up to the store window and looked in to check the lines. She sighed in annoyance. It was only a little past four, too early for the Friday-after-work crush, but the place was jammed.

She stayed there for a minute, trying to decide what to do. If she went in, she'd be on line so long she'd miss her walk. But if she shopped at the little place on the Lake Road, she'd get inferior groceries at tourist prices, even at this time of year. A few pieces of chicken and some salad greens, and she'd need a bank loan.

What the heck. If it was a question of missing her exercise or paying extra, she'd pay. She'd been sitting down all day. Her part-time job at the Lakeside Fitness Center required her to lead eight aerobics classes a week, but she hadn't had one today; all she'd done was paperwork. She'd go buggy if she had to get ready for company without unwinding.

She went to the Marina Market, got her groceries and a bottle of wine, remembered cat food as she was paying, ran back for it and was through in ten minutes. Good. It was worth the money, even though the chicken cost as much as lobster and seemed to have been grown with extra, undesirable appendages previously unknown to biologists.

She went back along the Lake Road toward home. A low whitish fog veiled the water; fortunately, it seemed to stay there. The road was clear.

She turned into Crestview a little too fast, eager to put on her jeans and parka and get outside. Immediately she had to brake to a stop, skidding slightly on the snowy road. Two police cruisers were blocking the way, pulled up head-to-tail so their occupants could shoot the breeze.

She waited a minute, but they showed no sign of moving. Frustration surged. Automatically, without thinking, Ruth hit the horn, a demanding blast that rang loud in the quiet whitened neighborhood. She could see the two policemen's heads spin her way in surprise.

Oh, good grief. She should have known. One of them was Frank Gordon.

The chief wasn't wearing his sunglasses today, so there was nothing to obscure the murderous look he shot her. He said something to the other man, who drove off. Then he simply sat there and let Ruth steer the Toyota around him. She drove with her eyes fastened on the road, refusing even to glance his way. Her flesh still prickled at the venom in his face. And her heart was beating very, very fast.

Frank watched in his rearview mirror as Ruth continued along Crestview to her building. She turned into the driveway that led to the lot in back.

Even though the Toyota was gone from his sight, he still watched the mirror, looking for he knew not what. The heel of his hand hurt where he'd banged it on the dashboard in anger when Ruth blew the horn. Wouldn't you know the obnoxious woman couldn't wait thirty seconds for police business to be completed.

Of course, the police business in this particular case happened to be the spaghetti-and-beer blast Phil and his wife Debbie were throwing tomorrow night for the force, but what was the difference? She didn't know that, and anyway, department morale was as important an issue as anything.

He looked away from the mirror and found himself doing the damnedest thing. He'd brought the cuff of his jacket to his nose and was taking a sniff. He dropped his arm as though it had been bitten, but not before Ruth Barrett's strong, sexy perfume had filled his nostrils.

He hadn't been able to get the smell out of the leather; he'd just have to wait until it dissipated on its own. For the time being he'd taken to keeping it in the car, willing to tolerate the New Hampshire chill between the station parking lot and the building rather

31

than have the men making remarks. One more thing to thank Ruthless for. The lady was poisonous.

He realized he was looking at the mirror again, and suddenly he knew why. He was waiting for her to come out. He wanted to see her run off, the way she had the other day, her slim, tight body pumped and flying. He wanted another look at those long, long legs, the yellow hair that had felt so silky in his hand, the peach-smooth skin.

He grunted in disgust at himself, shifted, and took off.

"Dinner was great last night," Joan Lindsay said, moving her laundry basket to rest it on her lean hip. "What did you do to the chicken? I meant to ask then, but we got on to something else."

"Oh, I just sprinkled Worcestershire sauce on it, and garlic powder. And I put a little wine in the pan, to have something to baste with. Nothing you wouldn't approve of," Ruth said, smiling at her neighbor. "In fact, you might want to give the recipe to your Pounds Off group."

"I do want to. It was delicious. Chris hated to miss it."

"Too bad he couldn't come."

"I know. But he'd never skip basketball practice, even for a good dinner. It was nice of you to invite him, especially since you see so much of the kids around here." She lifted a blue-jeaned leg to rebalance the basket. "You always seem to be finding jobs for them, or organizing ballgames, or solving their problems. I don't spend half as much time with teenagers, and I *have* one. Don't you ever OD on them?"

"Not usually," she said, pulling on her gloves. "Teenagers are fun. They're so direct. They haven't learned to be polite yet."

Joan wrinkled her nose. "Sometimes I can't wait until Chris does. Anyway, have a good run."

"It's hard without the hill."

"Oh, right. That chief is a real creep. How could he do that to you? He should have told the old man to let you through. You weren't hurting anything."

"Nothing but his macho pride," Ruth said.

"He sounds like a monster." Her narrow high-cheekboned face tightened. "Believe me, I know how frustrating it is to deal with these men. Chris is always telling me how the police hound his friends. They're all power-crazy. And it's even worse now than ever, with the muggings. They pick on the kids unmercifully —as if that'll do anything about the crime rate."

The two women said their good-byes, then Ruth went outside and down Crestview, starting from a moderate jog to warm up. Now that she no longer had her uphill start, she'd have to pace herself completely differently. Geary Street or the Lake Road—which way should she go? The Lake Road, she decided. Geary had a little bit of a grade, but it was boring. At least the Lake Road would give her a couple of peeks at the water through the trees.

She ran down the Lake Road, increasing her speed until she'd slipped into a steady rhythm. When she reached the track she wasn't even breathing hard. She'd have to get used to this now, to starting the course without having exerted herself. It didn't feel right at all.

But as always, the lake cheered her. She ran through the pines, breathing in their spice, careful to avoid the

33

patches of snow left from yesterday. Occasionally the rustle of a squirrel or bird broke the silence, but mostly there was no sound but the *pat-pat* of the water, the low wind, the pounding of her feet on the track.

She rounded a rocky hill and saw another runner way up ahead. She knew when she'd watched the man for a few seconds that she'd have no trouble getting the track back to herself again. He was jogging, but very slowly. Good. It was selfish to want to be alone here, but she did. There was nothing she liked less than to meet someone running at about her pace. Then she either had to speed up, or live with the uncomfortable sensation of having someone just behind or ahead of her for the whole run.

She saw as she came closer that the man wore a gray sweatshirt and dark pants, and was moving in a rather ungraceful non-rhythm. He was tall, very tall. The distance between them got smaller. She was only twenty yards from the man now. He sure was huge. He wore no hat, and his light-brown hair was blowing in the . . .

Light brown hair. *Sandy* brown. It couldn't be.

She raced a little to catch up. She reached him and turned to see his face. It was Frank.

"It's you," she said, running alongside him on the track.

He looked at her. He didn't seem nearly as surprised as she felt.

"So," he said, puffing. "Come here often?"

Ruth took her eyes off the track again to gape at him. Was he actually bantering with her?

Her vigilance interrupted, she tripped on a pine root. "Oh, no!" she cried as she went sprawling off the track. She slid on her front down the embankment, grabbing for a handhold. Her fingers touched the slim trunk of a shrub, but thorns dug into her palm when she tried for a grip, and she let go with a howl.

This isn't happening, she thought as she felt herself in air for an instant before she hit the water.

It was colder than anything she'd ever known. She gasped without opening her mouth, and water rushed into her nose. She thrashed desperately for the surface.

Her face broke through, but only long enough for her chin to get bumped by an ice chunk. She had a bare second to begin a gulping breath before the weight of her sweats drew her down. She kicked out, feeling for something, anything, to propel herself up again—but there was nothing.

Panic shot through her. She was going numb. Very soon she wouldn't be able to move anymore.

But suddenly her wrist was in a vise, and a second later she had air, lovely air. She blew out through her nose, not caring. The ground was half snow, half frozen scrub under her stomach. She looked up. Frank Gordon was crouched beside her.

"Yuck," she said, and turned her head away.

"So it lives," he said. "Come on. I have a blanket in the car." He grabbed her waist and hefted her to her feet as if she were weightless.

"You have to be d-dreaming," Ruth said. She coughed, and wanted to blow her nose again. The chief dug a handkerchief from his sweatshirt pocket and held it out, but she ignored him and reached for the tissues in her own pocket. Of course, they were mush. She felt like an idiot. She began to shiver, and in a second her teeth were chattering.

The chief glared down at her. Even in the mismatched sweats he looked as solid and authoritative as he did in uniform. His brown eyes were determined and angry.

"I could leave you here and let you die of hypothermia," he said, "but that would just get the department in more trouble than you've gotten it into already. Let's go." He took her arm.

Ruth was freezing and terribly weak. It was a huge effort to wrench away.

"Just exactly where," she demanded in a small, shaky voice, "do you think I'm going?" Her body was quaking madly from the chill of her soaked clothes and no doubt from shock. She'd almost drowned in the lake, and her limbs had quickly become nearly useless from the cold. There was no question that she'd badly needed Frank's help then, and she needed it now.

But something in her was revolted by the idea that she was just supposed to follow this big strong policeman wherever he said. Wasn't it his fault that she had fallen in the lake to begin with?

"I wouldn't have tr- tr- tripped if it hadn't been for you," she managed.

Frank Gordon looked at her in exasperation. "You're right. I give you that. Does it make you feel better? Now, let's get the hell out of here and warm you up before you expire on me."

He reached for her again, but stopped. She was shivering harder, and her face had lost more color. He'd better not wait to get her to the car. He had to bring her temperature up now.

He stepped behind her, took hold of the bottom of her sweatshirt, and yanked upward. It had a thick thermal lining that was heavy with lake water, and she wore only a T-shirt under it. He threw the sodden weight aside and pulled off the shirt. She must have had an adrenaline surge, because she came alive suddenly, wriggling and yelling.

"You lunatic!" she shouted. "Are you insane? Why are you undressing me?"

"Oh, stop complaining," he yelled back. "I just dragged you out of a freezing lake, and now I've got to get these clothes off of you before you turn into a blond icicle." But she'd spun to face him, and whatever modesty he'd tried to preserve was gone.

He couldn't take his eyes away. All the terrain he'd seen in his imagination was in front of him, and he felt himself warming as he looked. Her skin was all goose bumps, but she was lovely still, her firm breasts jutting beneath the wet bra she didn't need. Her hair hung in gold strings on smooth, feminine shoulders. Her scent was all around her, powerful even though she'd been under water, the sweet, sensuous fragrance pulling at him, making his heart beat faster.

Quickly he stripped off his own sweatshirt to put on her, but she didn't see. She was grabbing for her wet one, still screaming at him. God, she was obstinate! How could a woman who smelled that nice and looked that great be such a pain?

"What kind of policeman *are* you? A few days ago you couldn't stand the sight of me, and now you're ripping my clothes off!"

Then she caught sight of Frank's naked chest, and swallowed hard. Fit or not, the man was beautifully built. Her body was still trembling, but not just from the cold.

She heard someone approaching on the track.

"What's the trouble here?" A runner stopped, a man about her size with a sculpted mustache. He wore

37

a perfectly styled black jogging suit. He looked from one to the other of them—at Ruth in soaked sweat pants and lace bra, her skin half white, half red from her screaming; at Frank bare from the waist up, an unending expanse of hairy chest beneath shoulders the width of a Pontiac.

"No trouble," Frank said. He stepped toward Ruth to put his shirt on her, but she leaped back, swatting at him.

"Get *away!*" she yelled.

He took her wrist. "Damn you, I only want—"

"Now, hold on just a minute!" the stranger said.

"Beat it, friend, will you?" Frank said.

Ruth tried to shake free of Frank's grip, but it was impossible. The man's fingers were like steel.

He said, "Hell, lady, you're strong. Will you relax?"

The stranger pushed in between them. "Let's take it easy, now. Real easy. I'm a psychologist," he told Frank. "What's your first name?"

"Chief," Frank said, deadpan.

"Chief. Uh-huh. Native American, are you? Interesting. Take a few slow, deep breaths, Chief, and let's see if we can't tame those violent feelings down a—"

"That's enough, Freud. Go do your act on some other lake," Frank said. "Lady, you're going to pass out in another minute. Come here."

He reached again to put his sweatshirt on her, and she grabbed it and slapped at his face with it.

"Ouch!" he bellowed as the zipper scratched his nose.

Seeing his opportunity, the stranger jumped on Frank's back and hung there, his arms around the thick neck. "Run!" he told Ruth.

"No, you don't," Frank said, taking her arm and

38

unloading the man in one easy motion. "Mister, I've had it with you. Get out of here."

"It's only fair to warn you—I'm trained in hand-to-hand combat."

"I'm terrified," Frank said. "Get *lost.*"

"This is your last chance. Let go of the woman or I'm calling the police."

Frank sighed. "I am the police."

"You're a policeman? I don't believe you."

"It's true," Ruth said. She wanted nothing more than to get this horrible farce over with, put her shirt back on and stop shivering and chattering. "I can take care of myself. I'm okay, really."

The man studied her. "Hostage syndrome," he muttered to himself. "Victim identifying with her attacker."

"Attacker!" Frank yelled. "Listen, clown, you don't know a criminal from a speckled trout. Don't—"

"I told you, I'm a psychologist," he said. "I'm quite qualified to—"

"You're qualified to shag out of here, and you'd better do it fast. Take your mustache and go, before I—"

"Wait," Ruth said. A picture had just come into her mind, the image of a gnarled old man pointing a rifle at her stomach while a certain policeman she knew said, "You'll be lucky if I don't buy him some bullets."

"You're right," she told the stranger. "You're very clever to see through him."

The slight man beamed. "I thought so. I—"

"Hold it!" Frank roared. Ruth jumped. She'd never heard anything that loud. "What the hell are you pulling now? I ought to throw you back in!"

"Hurry!" Ruth said. "Quick, go get help."

The man turned and started to run back along the track. "The hell!" Frank said, and took off after him. But it was useless; he was out of sight fast. Frank jogged back, breathing hard, his naked chest heaving.

But already Ruth was beginning to regret her impulsive act of revenge, her chilled and sodden mind slowly clearing as her body warmed. She realized that he was right; he *had* saved her life. Now he was only continuing to be helpful, in his own granite-footed way.

Contritely she began, "I might have been too hasty—"

But he wasn't about to listen. "Stuff it," he said wearily. He picked up his gray shirt, and in a lightning-like move he looped it around Ruth's upper body, then tied several knots so that she was lassoed and her arms were imprisoned. While her mouth was still open in a gasp of astonishment, he hefted her over his bare shoulder and carried her off.

"You try to kick me," he said, taking her through the trees toward the road, "and I'll tie your feet too."

"Drink this," Frank told her.

"Is it tea? I hate tea."

"Just drink it."

Ruth took a sip and made a face.

"You can stand it. You're a big girl. Finish it."

She leaned over and put the cup on the coffee table, holding the blanket around her shoulders. "It has to cool. I'll have second-degree burns."

He picked it up and handed it back to her. "It doesn't warm you if it isn't hot," he said as if speaking to a small but annoying child.

She clenched her teeth against the chattering, and when it eased she drank some more tea.

"I thought they gave brandy for this," she said.

"Maybe they do, if they have some. I don't. Tea is it. Tea or beer."

"Why does a big macho cop like you have tea in the house?"

"Why," he asked pleasantly, "would a dainty little muffin like you rather swig brandy?"

She rolled her eyes.

"Aren't you getting tired of this?" he asked. He sat on the couch, as far as possible from where Ruth sat buried in the blanket. "I am."

"Tired of what?" she asked evasively.

"God, Ruthless, do I have to spell everything out for you? Let's bury the hatchet, why don't we?"

She looked at him. He'd put on well-worn tan corduroys and a dark brown sweater. He'd insisted she wear the gray sweatshirt; it was the heaviest thing he had. His dark eyes were warm. He had a broad cleft chin that she hadn't paid attention to before.

When she didn't answer, he said. "Okay, how about this? Let's be civil on a trial basis. No commitments. If it doesn't work out, we can go back to trashing each other. I zap you, you zap me. Until one of us gets arrested or killed, anyway. What do you say?"

Ruth thought, *If anyone had told me a week ago that I'd be held at gunpoint with the police chief practically cooperating; that I'd be pulled from the lake by the police chief after falling in because of him; that I'd be carried by the police chief over his shoulder like a sack of cantaloupes; and that I'd then actually consider taking the police chief up on his offer of friendship, because despite everything he had a nice cleft in his chin and nice eyes and . . .*

The whole thing was mystifying. Mostly what she'd felt for Frank Gordon so far was a strong urge to kill, or at least maim. But other emotions were intruding more and more. She didn't know how he could attract her. But he did.

"Okay," she said.

He grinned. He watched as she reached through the blanket to push her still-damp hair out of her face. Even huddled under plaid wool, nothing showing but her longish nose, dimpled chin, and candid eyes, she was great to look at. Pretty, but something more: appealing, tantalizing. God knew why after all that had happened, but he wanted to know her better—to talk to her, sit with her, feed the hungry tickle that was there whenever he looked at her.

He remembered how she'd been a half hour ago in her wet lacy blue bra. What he'd really wanted to do, instead of wrestle her into his shirt, was grab her with both hands, hold her close, and hug the chill away.

He forced the notion out of his head. More of that and he'd jump her right now. Talk about your square one.

A thought occurred to Ruth. "You must have decided to take my advice," she said suddenly.

"What?" he asked. "What advice?"

"About your fitness. I was surprised to find you on the track. I could tell, uh . . . I mean, you probably aren't in the habit of . . ."

"That track's treacherous," he said. "Look what happened to you. I was keeping my pace down on purpose. Hey, guess what?"

"Hmm?"

"You stopped shivering."

42

"Oh. So I did." She tossed her head back to free it from the blanket.

"More tea?"

"I knew you were going to say that."

He stood up. "I'm not trying to torture you, you know."

"You aren't *now.*"

"Ruthless—"

"Wait," she said. "Forget that. It was a reflex. Will you stop calling me Ruthless?"

"If you'll keep your claws in."

"I'll t-try."

He peered at her. "I'm making you more tea."

"Please, no. I'll stop."

"Don't be stupid," he said, going into the kitchen. She heard him run water into the kettle, get out a cup, open the cabinet for a tea bag. "It's an involuntary reaction. You can't stop it."

"Yes, I can," she said. She clenched her teeth and tensed all her muscles. The shivering stopped. She relaxed, and it started again. Damn him.

"Maybe you'll be happier with another kind," he called from the kitchen. "I'm giving you Red Zinger."

"What did I have before?"

"Sleepytime. It's a chamomile blend. Listen, how about a sandwich? You must be hungry. I am."

Suddenly she was. "Okay. Thank you."

"Tuna, or tuna?"

"Uh, tuna."

"Good choice."

The kettle whistled. He brought her the tea and went back into the kitchen.

She looked at it. "It really is red," she said.

"Yes, it is. Drink it."

She ignored it and snuggled into the couch, pulling the blanket tight.

He called, "*Now*, babe, before it gets cold."

She picked up the cup and sniffed it with distaste. "How did you know I hadn't had any?"

"Cop's instinct. I'll be in there in one minute and I want to see the cup empty."

"All right," she grumbled, "but I'll have to come back to it. Where's the bathroom?"

"Around to your left. Third door."

When she returned to the living room, Frank was setting two plates on the coffee table. He handed her the cup.

"You weren't kidding about having beer in the house," she said with a note of awe. "But what do you do when you want to shower?"

"What? Oh, the beer in the bathtub. That's for to-night."

"Tonight?"

"A party. I said I'd bring the beer. For God's sake," he said, rising from the table, "do you think I keep cases of beer on ice in my bathtub just for myself?"

"Considering what else I've seen you do so far," Ruth said mildly, "that would be one of your more run-of-the-mill characteristics."

"Oh? Well, even if it was for me, even if I planned to drink it all *tonight*, that's better than being the kind of health freak who doesn't want anyone else to have a good time if she can't."

"Is that what you think?" Ruth said. "It so happens I like to have a good time just as much as—"

"Well, you sure could have fooled—"

"—don't have to overindulge to—"

"Hold it!"

44

Startled, she was quiet.

"Just for the hell of it," he said, "let's try an experiment. Let's see if we can actually communicate for fifteen minutes without getting into an argument."

"Well, it wasn't my fault you—"

"*Wait.* Here. Eat your sandwich. Maybe if your mouth is busy, I'll be able to finish a sentence."

Ruth eyed the plate he'd handed her. The sandwich was about two cups of tuna salad, swimming in mayonnaise, on Italian bread slices the size of Frisbees. She took a tentative bite from the edge. It was impossible to get much of the enormous sandwich in her mouth.

"As part of the experiment," he said, "we each have to say something friendly. I'll start. How about going to this party with me?"

"Tonight? The beer party?"

"I didn't call it a beer party."

"What kind is it, then?"

"Actually, it's a, uh, beer and spaghetti party."

Ruth immediately thought of several responses, ranging from comments on the carbohydrate level to a simple "Ugh," but before she could make one, Frank said, "*Your* friendly statement can be an answer to my friendly question."

"Oh. You mean like 'yes'."

"That's right." Fleetingly he wondered how that would work, Ruth Barrett at a party with wall-to-wall cops. They'd figure out who she was soon enough. Chief Gordon with a woman would attract attention anyway, since he never brought dates to parties, and the fact that it was Ruth would be the cherry on the sundae; his men would expect him to take out a contract on her, not bring her to a party. In fact, he wasn't sure himself how he'd progressed from hating her

45

guts to not wanting her out of his sight. But he'd asked her—it was too late to change that—and he was surprised at how much he wanted her to say yes.

Ruth saw a tomato slice peeking from her sandwich and pulled it out. Unobtrusively she wiped some of the mayonnaise off before taking a bite.

She looked up at Frank. "Wouldn't I be awfully unwelcome?"

"I'll protect you. I think I'm big enough."

She thought for a minute. "Okay," she said, her smile almost shy. "That'll be nice. I'd like to go."

"Really?"

"Really."

He finished his sandwich in a few quick bites and wiped his hands. Ruth looked so nice sitting there on his couch, wrapped in a blanket. She shivered now and then, but her color was better. Once she had more nourishment in her, she should be all set. But most of her sandwich was still left.

"You're not eating," he said.

She shrugged. "I'm not that hungry."

"You said you were. Is something wrong with the tuna?"

"Not really."

He looked her in the eye. "That's not the same as no."

"It's a little heavy on the mayo for me."

"Good grief. Ruthless—"

"Don't *call* me that," she said.

"Can you stop counting calories for three seconds?"

"I can stop, but maybe you should *start*. There's enough fat in one of these sandwiches to make your arteries get up and leave."

46

"Damn it, I'm not overweight!" he said. "Maybe five pounds at the most. I weight about what I did in college."

"How much is that?" she asked.

"I'm not sure, but—"

"Then how do you know—"

"I *know*."

"Do you have a scale?" she asked innocently.

"Not one I'm going to get on in front of you. You know, we still haven't made it through fifteen minutes."

She laughed. "Maybe we'll do better tonight."

"Either that or we'll be the entertainment."

"Speaking of that, what time is the party?" she asked.

"Seven."

"Wow. I'd better be getting home," she said. "I still have a lot of errands to do. If I can work up the energy. I feel so tired."

"Well, you ought to. People don't bounce right back from dangerous degrees of exposure," he said.

"Will it go late, do you think?"

He laughed. "Not a shot. Cops are real stiffs. We never do anything past ten that doesn't involve a toothbrush and a pillow."

"Really?" she said. "I thought you were all big party guys."

"A myth. We don't say, 'Okay, buddy, where's the fire?' either."

He put their dishes in the sink, got a jacket, and gave Ruth one. It hung to her knees. On their way out he glanced at the closet where he thought his scale was buried under some old papers. Now she'd made him curious. When he got back from taking her home, maybe he'd haul it out.

47

CHAPTER THREE

"Don't you ever wear skirts?" Frank said when she opened the door.

Hurt, Ruth glared. "You look nice too."

"Sorry. Close the door, will you?" he said, still standing out in the hall.

"What?" she said.

"Close the door."

She did. He knocked on it again. She opened it.

"Ruth!" he said, grinning. "Great to see you. That sweater looks terrific with your hair."

She laughed. He came into the foyer, a spacious area decorated in rose and royal blue that she used as her office. There was a white desk with a ballet print over it, and a small soft-looking sofa. A milk-glass lamp hung over the desk on a gold chain.

Actually, it was nice to see him too. His strong-jawed good looks were set off by his gray-and-tan plaid shirt. And extra pounds or not, he sure had a sexy build.

He'd been walking through her thoughts all afternoon. That had surprised her—and so had the eagerness with which she'd looked forward to going out with him. A police party? After she'd been quoted as saying half the force was overweight? And why did she want to go anywhere with Frank? Part of her was still angry at him.

Even so, she'd gotten ready with more fussing than she had in a long time, trying on three outfits before settling on the butter-colored sweater and cream wool pants.

"You really do look pretty," he said, touching her cheek. "I don't know why I said that." He did know; he wanted to see her legs, in hose or out, but not covered once again by pants.

"Peaches, no," Ruth said as a fluffy orange cat ran past them and into the kitchen. She went and got the animal, grateful for the distraction. The spot on her face where he touched her felt hot. He'd never touched her before in any way that wasn't mean or restraining, and the feeling was quite strange.

"I left some cheese on the counter," she explained, putting the cat down. "That's what she was after. She's like a vacuum cleaner with food. She'll eat anything."

"Well, she's found her soulmate," Frank said, watching the cat stretch up along his pants leg. He picked her up. She immediately rolled onto her back in his arms and gazed at him expectantly. He stroked her belly with a hand almost bigger than she was. The motorboat buzz of her purr could have been heard on the street.

Ruth watched his gentle stroking with fascination. She pictured herself arching in his arms the way the cat was, Frank looking down at her . . .

"I love animals," he said. "Sometimes when Bill Massey is on another assignment—he's the K-9 Unit guy—I take care of the dog. Ready to go?"

She turned away. It wasn't easy. "As soon as I throw a few things in my purse."

49

She went into her bedroom and came out with her coat. She turned on her answering machine. Frank took the coat and helped her into it; then he went to the machine and turned it off.

"You're with me tonight," he said. "I don't want anybody leaving messages on my time."

Ruth opened her mouth to argue, but found herself closing it without saying a word.

Frank drove out of Lakeboro and got onto the Region Bypass, the highway that would take them around the many small lakefront towns to Donald Bay on the opposite shore.

It was strange to be in his big old Lincoln as a willing passenger rather than a trussed object, Ruth thought. She'd had so many conflicting experiences with this man in only one day. She wondered what he was thinking. Probably much the same thing she was, she just knew it.

"What are you thinking?" she asked.

"About the beer. If I brought enough."

So much for ESP. "It looked like you had enough for the entire American League."

"In the tub? That wasn't all of it. I had six more cases on the back porch. I wanted those to be extra-cold."

"I guess it's a bigger party than I thought."

He shrugged. "Twenty, twenty-five people."

"They must be very thirsty people."

"Well, beer is what most everyone drinks." He glanced her way and smiled. "Everyone but my date, probably. Tab on the rocks with a twist?"

"No," she protested. "I'm not that boring."

"You'll have a couple of beers?"

"Well, I don't like beer, but I do drink."

"Wine?"

"Martinis."

"Martinis?" he repeated, as if she'd said "paint thinner." That was something. Ruth drinking martinis was as likely as—well, as Ruth wearing that powerfully alluring perfume that filled his car right now. For a second he flashed back to the morning, their struggle by the water and the surprising strength she showed. He wondered if she made love that way, with the same passionate energy.

He saw the sign for Donald Bay. Good thing they were almost there. He didn't want to be thinking such erotic thoughts while driving on a high-speed bypass. It would be kind of nice to get them to the party alive.

"Do you think nice girls don't?" she asked.

"Don't?" It came out sort of strangled, and he cleared his throat. "Oh. You mean drink martinis."

She glanced at him. "Isn't that what we're talking about?"

It's what one of us is talking about, he thought. "I'm not sure if Phil and Debbie have gin and vermouth. Like I said, this is a very quiet crowd. Cops are dull. Our idea of a hot time is throwing some extra nuts in the brownies."

They drove through the darkened streets of Donald Bay. The afternoon sun had erased the last traces of snow; the moon cast its pale pearly light across the bits of the lake Ruth could see through the trees. Frank pulled into the driveway of a dark-shingled Cape Cod house. Cars lined both sides of the street around it.

He opened the door for her and went to the trunk. He pulled out a giant cooler and carried it to the house as though it were a box of tissues.

A big-bellied man with dark hair and heavy eyebrows opened the door. "Hi, Frank," he said. "Let me have that. Is there more in the—oh!" His eyes widened in surprise as he caught sight of Ruth behind Frank.

Oh, no, Ruth thought, *does he recognize me?* She hoped not. She was jittery enough just being with Frank, liking him, wanting him to like her as much, trying to ignore their crazy beginning. And having to meet his friends on their first date wasn't exactly relaxing either. She'd wanted to get a little bit comfortable before having to worry about being found out.

To her relief, Frank took over. He seemed to have decided to meet the problem head-on. This was the first time she'd had reason to be pleased with his habit of doing that.

"Let me introduce you," he said, squeezing Ruth's waist. "Phil Davids, this is—"

"Happy birthday, Frank," another man said, coming outside. He clapped Frank on the back. "Five more years to the half-century mark. How does it feel?"

"Today's your birthday?" Ruth asked.

"Yesterday." He seemed embarrassed. He dropped his hand, and she immediately missed its promising warmth. "I didn't think anybody knew. How did you find out?"

The man shrugged. He looked at Ruth. "You brought a date?"

"We didn't think you would," Phil Davids said. "You never do."

"Well, I did tonight," Frank said firmly. "Why don't you two bring in the rest of the beer? We'll go inside and find Debbie, and I'll make introductions all around."

"Debbie's, uh, at her mother's," Phil said.

"What?" Frank asked, frowning. "How come?"

"We—it's— Never mind. I'll explain later. Go on inside," he said.

Frank looked hard at him for a minute. Then he led Ruth inside with a hand at her waist again.

"That's strange," he said. "I wonder if they're having a fight."

"Has this happened before?" Ruth asked.

"Never."

"Do you think he recognized me?" she said. "I couldn't tell for sure."

"I wasn't sure, either. But if he did," Frank said, smiling, "you'll be livening up the party by giving them something to talk about. Nothing as exciting as this ever happens."

They went into the living room. It was a large but cozy area with love seats and armchairs upholstered in garden prints, and a thick brown carpet. There were bowls of snacks on every table. Guests stood around in laughing groups.

About what she'd expected to see. But there was something wrong. What was it?

Three things happened simultaneously at that moment. Everyone in the room turned to look curiously at her. The doorbell rang. And Ruth realized what was odd: she was the only woman in the room.

"Frank!" Phil called from the foyer. "Answer the door!"

Frank scowled. "Me?"

"Yes!" Phil said. He motioned him to come. "The bell just rang. Answer it."

The room had gone quiet. All the men were watching Frank, some glancing at Ruth. She hadn't the remotest idea what was going on, but she felt like a mouse at a cats' convention.

Everyone seemed to be waiting for Frank to open the door, even though Phil was actually standing closer to it.

Looking confused, Frank finally went to the door and opened it.

Ruth heard someone screech, "Happy birthday!" and then a giant chicken was hugging Frank, pulling his head down to kiss him with its pointy beak.

"What the hell?" he shouted.

The chicken released him, turned around, and pushed a button on a box just inside the door. Loud music with a deep booming rhythm filled the house. Then the chicken grabbed Frank's hand and pulled him into the living room as everyone backed away to make a path.

Ruth thought, *Am I going crazy?* She continued stepping back after the men had stopped, until she was against a wall, able to see what was happening but definitely on the sidelines. A few of the men looked uneasily at her and then back to the action.

Gyrating to the music, the chicken danced around Frank, as seductive as a five-and-a-half-feet-tall feathered creature can be. Ruth saw him look for her, and when he caught her eye, she did her best to smile bravely. It was about as easy as smiling through oral surgery, and she must not have been very convincing, because his brow tightened in concern.

Now she felt worse. She didn't want Frank to think she was a bad sport, even if it meant looking enthusiastic while he danced with a lusty chicken. She'd just have to try her hardest to appear cool, despite the way her stomach was threatening to march out of her body.

The men, after a few last nervous glances in Ruth's direction, seemed to be getting into the spirit of the entertainment. They were clapping, moving to the beat.

The chicken pushed at its head and the thing came off, revealing a lovely feminine face framed by dark curls, beautifully made up in shiny show-biz colors. She tossed the headpiece over her shoulder and one of the men caught it and put it on.

She continued to dance while she pulled a long feather from her back slowly, with disco-beat rolls of her chicken's bottom. When it was out she raised it triumphantly and everyone cheered. She began to tickle Frank with it, running it teasingly across his face and flicking it behind his ears. She did a little shimmy in back of him, and when he heard the noise the men made, he turned around. She poked the feather inside his shirt and then quickly pulled it out before he could protest.

Ruth's smile felt like it was turning to cement. She would have given anything to be able to disappear. She pressed herself against the wall and prayed to be absorbed into it.

So it wasn't recognition that had caused Phil Davids and the other man to behave so strangely when they saw her. It was the fact that Frank had brought a woman to a stag party that was really his birthday surprise.

The dancer dropped the feather and whipped off the remaining three pieces of the bulky costume, throwing them into the crowd. Laughing, the men who caught them passed them to the one wearing the chicken head, and he put them on.

Now she wore a spangled red-and-green bodysuit

that caught the light and threw sparks of color as she danced. The beat had grown stronger and she gyrated around Frank, tossing her dark curls. Saucily she darted toward him and away, keeping time with the music's throb.

Her hands went to her chin. Some in the group obviously knew what came next, because a roar was building, and a moment later her bodysuit top was off and she was dancing in tights and a glittering bra top with fringe that swung as she moved. She smiled at Frank and the men and danced faster.

Dear Cosmo, Ruth thought desperately, *I have a problem. What do you do when a beautiful woman with feathers and a beak starts doing a striptease for your date?*

The whole room was caught in the music and the seductive rhythm of the dance. The woman kicked high, and bracelets jangled on her ankles. Her face had a damp sheen that highlighted her lovely, exotic features. She circled Frank with her back to him, holding her arms high and clapping, urging the crowd to clap louder, harder.

Frank tried again to catch Ruth's eye. He'd been glancing her way constantly, hoping to shoot her a reassuring look. He was mortified; he could only imagine how she must feel. But she seemed too dazed to realize he was trying to send her a message.

Poor Ruth. She'd come bravely to the party, knowing she might get a cool reception. He'd never have guessed what would actually happen—that *he* would get a *hot* one!

For however many more excruciating minutes this circus lasted, he had to go with it; he knew his guys, knew how much planning and money must have gone into his birthday treat. He couldn't ruin things for his men. But what would Ruth think of them—Ruth, who hadn't started out a big fan of the police department anyway—or of him?

When the clapping and shouting were nearly as loud as the music, the dancer looked around, smiled again, and wriggled out of her tights. Now she wore only bikini bottoms with the bra top. She threw the tights high in the air and one of the men, a bald one with a heavy middle, put them on. There were howls of laughter as he began imitating the dancer's bumps and grinds.

Another man picked up the big feather she'd dropped. When her dance brought her near him, he reached out and tickled her neck with it. Laughing, she spun around and grabbed it. In a motion quicker than the eye could see, without breaking the rhythm of her dance, she pushed the feather down the back of the man's shirt.

The crowd noise reached a swelling pitch and she let them wait, dancing around Frank some more, building tension for her finale.

Ruth thought, *I know what she's going to do next. I wish I didn't, but I do. Oh, please, let this be over. Please don't let her take her top off. Please let me look as if I'm handling this just fine. No, don't let her reach back there, don't—*

The dancer snapped off the bra top and threw it in the air. Small tasseled triangles covered her breasts, nothing more. Ruth put her hands over her eyes. The dancer moved faster than ever, keeping time to the beat that was now so rapid that the clapping sounded like one steady noise, a loud thrum of excitement that bonded the room to the performer.

She beckoned the men to enter the circle and join her. They went eagerly, dancing and laughing. She reached for the top button of Frank's shirt, and he must have decided to draw the line there, because the next thing Ruth knew she was being propelled through a swinging door into the relative peace of the kitchen by Frank's firm grip on her arm.

"God, Ruth, I'm sorry," he said. "I had no idea anything like this was going to happen. Are you okay?"

"Yes," she said. She was so glad it was over that she felt limp with relief.

"Some first date. You must think I'm a weirdo." He started opening cabinet doors. "Hold on. Don't go away. Ah, here."

He'd managed to come up with gin and vermouth and even a lemon, and he made her a martini and handed it to her.

"Thanks," she said. Her pulse was slowing at last. She tried to sound composed. "I've read that you can hire people to do that at parties, but I've never seen it."

"Were you horrified? Your face is the color of cranberry juice."

So much for her attempt at looking cool. "I, well . . ."

He laughed. "I was thrown, too." He opened a beer and took a long drink. "It was great of the guys to plan something. But I would have liked it better," he said, leaning down to kiss her ear, "if a couple of things had been different."

She wanted to touch the place where his lips, cool from the beer, had left an imprint that burned like flame.

"What couple of things?" she asked.

"The identity of the dancer—and the amount of company." He bent to her once more, and her heart hammered. This time his lips found hers, and the feeling was so sweet she sighed against his mouth. He tasted of beer and heat. She wanted to put her arms around him, but she didn't dare.

Then the swinging door opened, and Frank quickly straightened. The man in the spangled tights came into the kitchen. He now wore the bra top also, and no shirt.

"You're missing everything," he said, taking a huge armload of beer cans. "Yow. This stuff's cold."

He dashed back through the door, and Ruth caught it before it closed and looked into the living room. The stripper was dancing in the center of a group. The other dancers included the man in the chicken suit, the one with the feather sticking out of his shirt, a handful of men without shirts, and two in their shorts.

"Tell me again," she said over her shoulder to Frank, "about how this crowd's idea of a hot time is throwing some extra nuts in the brownies."

It was after one by the time they got to the Lakeboro exit and turned off the bypass onto the quiet town streets. They'd left the party as soon as they could and spent the rest of the evening listening to music at a Donald Bay nightclub. Ruth yawned, then yawned again, so widely her jaw cracked.

"You must be wiped out," Frank said.

"And this was going to be my relaxed Saturday," Ruth said dreamily. "Imagine. It started with my nearly drowning and ended with a strip show." She yawned once more. "I guess I won't be out on the track as early as usual tomorrow. How about you?"

"Me? No way," he said.

"You don't run every day?"

"I don't run, period. As you probably suspected."

She turned to look at him. Of course. Why hadn't she seen it? Out in February with no hat . . . unmatched, thrown-together outfit . . . shoes much too clean. She'd noticed all that without adding it up.

"So I made an impression!" she said. "You're beginning an exercise program."

He laughed. "You made an impression all right, but not the kind you mean. I was out there hoping to run into you. Literally. Which is pretty much the way it happened, except for that little problem with the lake."

She shivered slightly, reliving the little problem, then harder as she recalled Frank's naked chest. She remembered the huge shoulders, the way his arm and torso muscles bulged, the effortless strength of his grip. She'd been flirting with hypothermia, and still her body had been busy, exquisitely aware of the attraction between them.

And now he'd admitted that he felt the tug from the beginning too—so much so that he'd actually gotten suited up and pretended to be a regular runner. No wonder his car had been so conveniently near; for all she knew, he could have been jogging along the same short stretch over and over, waiting for her. She had no doubt that he meant it: he was drawn to her. But she also knew that the tensions that had marked the beginning of their relationship were still with them: the *Banner* article, his letting Mr. Zachariah terrorize her and then just mildly scolding him.

So the confrontation was still fresh; nothing had been resolved, and it didn't look as though anything would be. But without consciously making up her mind, she seemed to have decided to push the bitterness away—to go with her other feelings.

She never would have predicted she'd act this way—obeying her impulses, letting the tickle of fire in her body that appeared whenever she saw Frank or heard his voice rule her actions. It was radically unlike her to allow this enormous, arrogant man to call so many shots.

And he was clearly used to it. Frank Gordon did things his way, and that was that. But then again, she wasn't exactly a paragon of docile passivity, and she knew that he knew it.

Which meant that he was probably doing what she was: obeying his impulses.

"So," she said. "Your jogging by the lake. It was an ambush."

"Ambush. Yeah." In the car's shadowy dimness she saw his half-grin. "That's exactly what it was."

"There's one thing I don't understand," she said. "Why go to all that bother? Why didn't you just call me?"

They'd reached her building on Crestview. He pulled up in front and shut off the engine, then he turned to her, resting his arm along the top of the seat.

"I like to watch you run," he said.

Ruth swallowed. She couldn't think of anything to say. She imagined him watching her, in her sweats, her ugly sweats, with no makeup and her hair every which way. She thought she made a thoroughly unappealing picture, but apparently he didn't. From the way Frank was looking down at her, it was clear he had a very different opinion.

In the light of a streetlamp she could see his eyes, warmed with gold glints, regarding her with a kind of smoky hunger. His wide, shapely mouth was open a little, and was it her imagination that he was breathing faster?

He took some of her hair in his hand and tugged it gently. "The truth is," he said quietly, "I like to watch you do damn near anything. I called you Ruthless"—she started to speak, but he shushed her with another tug—"and I was teasing, getting you going, but it's true. You are ruthless—in what you do to me, anyway. I guess you can't help it. There's just something about you, babe, that heats me up like a furnace."

His hand slipped to her face and brought it close to his. Then his big soft mouth was on hers and his hand cradled her head, holding her there, just in case she had any ideas about pulling away.

It was the last thing on her mind. She kissed him back, willingly, eagerly. Her hands went to his shoulders and she ran her fingers across them and down his arms, feeling the cords of heavy muscle even through his wool jacket.

"Ruthless," he whispered. "You make me crazy."

He licked her mouth and then turned her face up so he could get at her neck. She felt his lips on the tender flesh there, and the soft scrape of his stubbled jaw. He kissed her under the chin, beneath her ear, and then on the mouth again. This time his tongue entered and found hers.

She moaned softly, and he pulled her closer. His hands were at her back, their pressure so strong it almost hurt. She could feel his longing in his touch, in his lips, in his harsh breathing.

He buried his hands in her hair and held her face a few inches from his. He looked at her for several seconds, at her eyes, her slightly swollen mouth, her dimpled chin. Then his lips went where his eyes had been. Ruth felt his soft tongue on her lashes, licking at the corner of her eye. It followed the side contour of her nose, tasted the little ridge above her upper lip, and descended to her chin, where it explored the cleft.

"I wanted to do that the second I saw you," he whispered.

She laughed softly. "Me, too." She touched his chin with her finger and then with her tongue.

He took the reins back immediately, covering her lips again with his insistent ones, feeling the satiny interior of her mouth with his possessive tongue. He opened her jacket, handling the thick zipper easily. He reached for the bottom of her sweater and an instant later his hands were on her skin, roughly stroking her back.

Ruth wound her arms behind his neck and kissed him deeply. Her skin where his hands were was coming alive, every inch responding to his urgent touch. She had to stop him, she knew that; they were right out in front of her building, and besides, the whole situation was confusing enough without her letting this progress any further.

But he was so warm and delicious. His big body *was* like a furnace, practically enveloping her in its fiery coals. The things his mouth was doing to her face, her ears, now her neck . . .

"Frank," she said. "We have to stop." She pushed against his chest. It was like resisting an eighteen wheeler.

He took her lips again, using his teeth. He pulled his hands from under her sweater to hold her head once more, and she had no choice but to stay with the kiss, let it carry her away. But a minute later she made herself come up for air. She *had* to.

"Frank," she said louder, and wriggled against him, hard enough to show she meant it. "Let go. Please. You've got to."

He dropped his hands slowly. He looked at her face once more, that same odd surveying gaze, as though trying to find answers there he didn't know where else to seek.

"I have to go in," she said.

He nodded. He zipped her jacket, pulling the tab to her chin, and opened his door.

"You don't have to walk me in. I'll be fine," she said quickly.

He didn't answer, just got out anyway and went to the front door of the building with her. She opened it with her key.

"Good night, Frank," she said. "It was . . . I liked being with you."

"I'll come to your door," he announced.

She gave up and went to the stairs. Just then Joan came down, carrying a pizza box. Because Frank was a few steps behind, she saw only Ruth at first.

"You out so late? I don't believe it," she said. "Where were you, on a midnight run? I've never—"

There was a sudden silence while Joan's gaze darted from Ruth to Frank and back again. Then once more to Frank.

"Isn't this the pol— I mean, wasn't he the one . . ." In a rare show of embarrassment, Joan looked down at the pizza box, flushing.

"Yes. And yes," Frank said when Ruth stayed silent. "Good night, now."

With a firm hand on Ruth's shoulder, he hustled her

past her neighbor and up the stairs. Ruth heard Joan continue on down to the garbage room after a moment. She had a mad impulse to call her back. Anything to prevent herself from having to be alone once more with this man and his totally confounding ability to make her feelings jump around like droplets on a griddle.

She put her key in her door. Her hand fumbled as she tried out sentences in her head, marshaling the arguments that would get her inside, alone, and him down the stairs and out, alone. Tactic number one, of course, was to be sure and avoid any further contact right now. If he so much as reached to shake her hand, she'd tell him there was no way on earth—

Warm lips on the back of her neck drove the rest of the thought completely out of her mind. Frank had pushed her hair away as she bent to turn the key and was kissing her. She straightened and turned to make it clear to him that—

Then his mouth was crushing hers again, the fiery tongue sweetly intruding, threatening to destroy her resolve. A few seconds passed, a brief time of agonizing rapture, while Ruth nearly went under. She was a breath away from letting him—no, *begging* him to come in with her, when some half-buried nugget of sense asserted itself.

"Frank, stop," she said. She heard footsteps. Oh, good grief; that was what had kept her from surrendering, her remembering somewhere in the back of what was left of her mind that what goes down must come up.

She wrenched away from Frank's arms just as the top of Joan's head appeared on the stairway. She stood, silently sorting through various idiotic phrases, while Joan hurried past, examining the wall opposite Ruth's door with tremendous interest.

"You have to go. *Now,*" Ruth said. "Don't you dare argue. I have no intention—"

"Okay," he said. "Sleep tight."

Ruth stared at him.

"What's the matter?" he asked. "Did you think you'd have to fight me off?"

"I—"

"Relax. You left the car with your virtue intact, didn't you?"

"Well, yes. But that was *my* doing."

He grinned. "So you think I backed off because you stopped me?"

She nodded.

He chuckled. The sound had a cruel edge. "Honey," he said as he started down the stairs, "if I hadn't intended to stop, you wouldn't have been *able* to stop me."

He left without even glancing back at her.

CHAPTER FOUR

"Is it too early?" Joan asked. "I couldn't wait."

"No," Ruth said, smiling into the phone. "I've been up for a while. I'm having coffee."

"Thanks, I was hoping you'd ask. I'll be right there," Joan said, and hung up.

The bell rang within seconds.

"Well?" she demanded when Ruth opened the door. "And if you say, 'Well, what?' I won't give you what I have in here." She held up a paper bag.

"What is it?"

"Devil Dogs."

Ruth laughed. "Come on in." She reached for the bag.

"Not yet," Joan said, clutching it to her. "Will you tell me what happened, or are you going to be your usual maddeningly discreet self? I couldn't believe that was Frank Gordon. Yesterday morning you couldn't talk about the man without looking as if you wanted to kill him. Then I find the two of you necking in front of your door. Anybody walking by could get scorched by the—"

"Okay," Ruth said, blushing.

"So?" Joan said encouragingly. They sat at the

67

kitchen table, and she unwrapped two of the chocolate-and-cream pastries.

Ruth took a bite of hers and chewed it for a long time before she answered. Finally she said, "I don't know."

Her eyes on Ruth's, Joan closed the box.

"I'm not being coy," Ruth said. "It's the truth. I really don't know how I got from hating him to—to—"

"Yes?" Joan leaned forward. Her short hair, as dark as Ruth's was blond, shone in the early sun that spilled through the kitchen window.

"Not hating him," she finished, shrugging.

Joan put the box back in the bag and stood up.

"Wait," Ruth said. "Let me try again. See, the crazy thing is, all of that is right. I *was* furious at him yesterday morning. I'm still mad. And we *were*, uh"—Joan closed the bag and held it when she hesitated—"uh, doing exactly what you said."

Joan's eyebrows went way up. She put the box back on the table and sat down.

Ruth laughed. "No, not that much. I mean, we—I guess you could say we moved past acting hateful to each other, and into something that could be—romantic." She picked up another Devil Dog, unwrapped it, licked frosting from her fingers, and took a bite. Peaches came in and leaped onto the table. Ruth put her firmly down. "But I'm not sure how I feel about it, any of it. And I haven't the haziest idea what *he* thinks."

"You haven't?" Joan said. "Why not? Just from my quick observation, I could give a good description—"

Ruth held up her hand. "I know how it looked. I was *there*, remember? All I can tell you is, the whole thing is confusing. He treated me horribly at Mr. Zachariah's; I still want to kill him. And I can't wait to see him again."

"Well, is it being too nosy—"

"Not that you care."

"True. Can I ask what exactly happened between yesterday morning and last night to change everything?"

Ruth sighed. She felt very weary suddenly. She didn't want to go into it all: her fall into the lake, Frank literally dragging her to his apartment, the party . . . it still seemed like an insane dream to her, so how could she explain it to someone else?

Then the phone rang, making them both jump, and as quickly as she'd felt tired, Ruth was energized again.

"That could be Frank," she said, knocking her chair against a counter as she ran to answer.

Joan smiled and shook her head as she left.

"Mail, Frank," Terry Daniels said. He dropped some envelopes and a magazine on the chief's desk. "Nice day, huh? Good to see the sun."

"Yeah," Frank said, glaring at the small pile of letters as though certain one of them contained a bomb.

Terry shrugged and left, closing the office door.

He went back to the pile of purchase orders he was working on. They didn't need nearly as much concentration as he was giving them, but he wanted to put off opening his letters. The mail had become something to dread the last few weeks, just as the phone was. Its peculiar burring ring had once seemed pleasant, the promise of a distraction from whatever routine work he was doing. He loved the unexpected, the charge of a new challenge dropping in his lap. Instant action and on-the-line decisions were what he liked most about police work, and he often answered the phone to find one of those situations waiting for him, like a wrapped present.

But lately the phone was maddeningly unpredictable. Sometimes it gave him just what he wanted, a chance to get out of the office and do his work. Other times, though, it only gave him a headache, or made the one he already had far worse.

It wasn't just the official types who were hassling him. Often he had to listen at least briefly while Mr. or Mrs. John Q. Citizen fed him their two cents about the department's "problem." And more of those calls were reaching him since last Saturday; the men weren't screening them out. It was their way of getting him back for bringing the enemy into their midst. Once word had gotten around the station about who the blonde at the party had been, the temperature in here had dropped about twenty degrees. Except for Phil and Terry, his closest friends, the chill was unmistakable.

He couldn't blame them, but it ticked him off just the same. At a time when he was getting flak from every direction, he could have used their support. Well, at least the men wouldn't have to doubt the chief's loyalty to the department again. He knew he should have resisted the impulse that had made him invite Ruth Barrett to the party. He should have left things the way they'd been after the fracas with the old man, both of them burning with hate. It had been stupid of him to go to the lake and then to take her to the party. His hormones had been eclipsing his brains. He'd make up for that now.

He finished with the last purchase order and moved another sheaf of paper work over and started on that.

The phone rang.

He cursed, let it go for five rings, and cursed again. He picked it up.

"Gordon," he growled.

"Frank?"

"Yeah."

"George Heck. Didn't recognize your voice."

"What's up, George?" He relaxed his grip on the phone. This call wouldn't be a problem. George was one of the few trustees who hadn't been on him about the weight thing.

"Thought I'd ask you to take a turn or two around that parking lot at Weirs Beach."

He felt a jolt of adrenaline. There was police work waiting to be done.

"I'll go right over. What's the trouble?"

"No, no. No rush," the trustee said. "Tonight would be better. There's usually no problem in daylight."

"What problem, George? Is there something that needs my attention, or not? You don't mean that old vandalism business, do you? We settled that."

"Well, we did and we didn't. The property owners around the lot are still complaining to my office."

"I don't know why," Frank said. "I tripled the patrol over there. We have hardly any incidents anymore." He reached across his desk for the pile of mail and opened the top envelope, inserting his finger and ripping it. There was a slim-bladed opener in a brass desk set in front of him, but he never used it, or any of the things in the set.

"Things still happen," George said. He sounded sheepish. "Kid threw a rock the other night."

"Hit anyone? Break anything?"

"No," George said.

"Well, what's the problem, then?" He opened another envelope, glanced at the fund-raising leaflet inside, and threw it into the wastebasket. "I've got men checking that lot every time somebody coughs. There's no more graffiti, no damage, no muggings around there. What do they want, an armed guard with a Doberman?"

"I don't know, Frank. They're just nervous. I think it would do a world of good if you could take a spin by there a night or two. Let the people see the car, reassure them you're on top of things."

"Come on, George. The men making rounds over there are on top of things just fine." He opened another envelope. "If it'll make the folks feel better, I'll have them blip the siren, flash the lights a little. Now, if that's all, I—"

"Actually, that isn't all. I don't think you get my meaning." He chuckled edgily. "The fact is—and, mind you, I don't share this view—people are uneasy. They're worried about the muggings. They want to know if everything's under control."

He pulled an ad out of the envelope, tearing it. "Under control? What the hell are you trying to say?" Automatically he fitted the halves of the ad back together. It wasn't an ad. It was a magazine picture of an oxygen tank. Across it someone had written, "Better order these for the cops so they can make some arrests."

"It's all this hoo-ha about the men being out of shape. Now, personally, I'd say the mugging problem can be solved pretty easily. You just have to lean on those kids. Really let them have it—show the little skanks you won't take any stuff off them. You do that, and I think the flak will die down when people see you mean business.

"But they're saying to me, if he can't control whether his own officers are fit or not, maybe he's not in charge, know what I mean? Like I said, *I* know you're as good as ever, but—"

"Damn it, George!" Frank yelled. He flung the picture away from him. The two pieces fluttered back onto the desk. He swept his arm across the surface, knocking everything near him onto the floor. "They don't know what the hell they're talking about! I'm sick and tired of being under fire for no good reason, just because a bunch of morons believe everything they read in the paper! Some fool of a prima donna athlete shoots her mouth off to a reporter, and all of a sudden I'm running an armed camp here!"

"I see your point, but Frank, you've got to admit, some of the men are awful big, and you can't—"

"Do you want us to look pretty," he roared, *"or do you want us to do our jobs?"*

He banged the phone down, grabbed his leather jacket, and stomped out.

"Could you possibly come sooner than Monday?" Ruth asked. "My tenant has water coming into her kitchen. I'm sure it's an ice dam—I've had them before in the building."

"I'm sorry, ma'am—I'm just the answering service," the woman said. "All I know is, he said Monday is the first day he has."

"Well, please ask him to call me as soon as he can, okay?" Ruth said. "Thanks."

She hung up and went to the window. The rain was

still heavy; vast gray curtains of it pounded the street. Foamy water streamed along the curb.

She'd taught only one aerobics class today; the other had been canceled because of the weather. That was all the exercise she was going to get. She couldn't run, and she couldn't even go back to the center and do anything there. She'd miss the roofer's call.

All in all, it was shaping up to be a crummy day.

She poured a glass of juice and sat at the table. There was plenty to do around the building and even in her apartment, but she didn't feel like doing it. The rain wasn't helping any, but she couldn't blame her mood on that; she was just down.

She finished her juice and put the glass in the sink. She wanted a shower, but the roofer would call for sure if she took one. Even if he left a message on her machine, it might take her forever to get him back.

Of course, if she didn't take a shower, he wouldn't call.

She glared at the phone. Stupid frustrating thing. It had been driving her batty lately.

For the first week that she hadn't heard from Frank, her throat had felt dry every time it rang. But that Sunday morning, when Joan had hurried out so she could talk to him, had turned out to be only the first of endless false alarms. By the second week, she'd taken to answering the phone with a resigned disappointment. Now, with the two-week mark day after tomorrow, she'd decided it was just as well. The thing with Frank was nutty anyway; in the short time she'd known him it had already turned into a roller coaster ride. Better to forget him now, before she had a lot invested in a relationship that was fated for anguish.

74

That was what she thought. What she felt was something else again.

The phone rang. She grabbed it before the ring had ended.

"Miss Barrett? Stan Richmond. Understand you have a water problem?"

She should have been relieved. Now she could get her problem solved, take her shower, leave the house if she wanted. But she was more disappointed than anything.

She arranged with the roofer to come that evening, called the tenant, and got undressed. She'd shower and go get her marketing done, now that she couldn't do it tonight.

She turned on the spray, stepped in, and closed her eyes, letting the soothing hot water splash over her head. Then she reached for her washcloth.

She couldn't find it. She opened her eyes, pushing her wet hair back. Rats. It was in the hamper.

She got out and went to the linen closet, hurrying, trying to drip as little as possible on the wood floor. She took a cloth.

The phone rang.

For a second she considered just letting the machine answer—but she couldn't. She picked it up.

"Ruth, I'm so glad you're home," Joan said, a note of panic in her voice.

She swallowed. "What's the matter?"

"It's Chris. He's not hurt, but he's terribly upset, and I'm frantic. He was at the lake when the rain started, cleaning up one of the picnic areas with some kids from school. Well, you know how it was, one minute there were a couple of clouds, and the next minute we had a downpour. They all ran home, and

Chris took the shortcut down Mr. Zachariah's road. He—"

"You're not going to tell me," Ruth interrupted, trying to dab some of the water out of her hair with the dry washcloth, "that the old lunatic pulled his gun?"

"He did! Chris was so scared, he just kept running. Maybe it wasn't loaded this time either, but so what? It's a terrible thing! He should be shot himself for pulling a rifle on a fourteen-year-old!"

Ruth threw down the cloth. "That monster! Did you call the police?"

"Of course I did. The man on the phone said they'd . . . *investigate.* I asked him, 'Are you implying that my son was at fault somehow?' Well, he completely side-stepped the question. He gave me some blather about not being able to say until they *investigated.* That's why I'm calling, Ruth. I hate to take advantage of your relationship with Frank, and you know I wouldn't ask if I wasn't beside myself—but could you call him?"

Ruth rubbed her forehead. She would rather run up the hill and arrest Mr. Zachariah herself than phone Frank Gordon, but Joan was right—the situation was intolerable. Something had to be done. Joan didn't know she hadn't been seeing Frank right along; it wasn't an unreasonable request. And she was furious herself. The fact that the police were dragging their feet was the final insult. She had to do it. Nobody, not even Frank, could be neutral on an issue like this. Threatening a child with a gun was horrible.

"I'll call him," she said. "Or—wait. I'm going to go over to the station and demand that they arrest that dangerous old man."

She said good-bye and grabbed her sweat pants from where she'd dropped them on the bed. She put them on, wincing as the cloth met her wet skin, but was too agitated to stop and dry herself. She pulled on her sweatshirt and hooded jacket, grabbed her car keys and purse, and ran to the door. She opened it, realized the noise she'd been ignoring was the running shower, ran back to turn it off, and hurried out to the car.

Trembling with anger, she shifted badly, grinding the gears. She screeched out of the parking lot and drove into town, her wipers fighting to keep up with the downpour.

She had to stop for a light on Main Street, and while she waited edgily for it to turn, she glanced at the rearview mirror. She hadn't thought about her appearance before dashing out, and she was shocked. Her hair stuck to her cheeks in damp ropes; her face was a disaster, half splotchy makeup, half clean streaks from the shower spray. And of course she was in her ratty sweats. She took a last look and drove on.

Well, too bad. She hated to face anyone looking so disreputable—least of all Frank Gordon and his department when she wanted to get action on an unconscionable breach of—

I'm an idiot. She took her foot off the gas and quickly stalled. Horns tooted behind her. She started the car again and pulled into a parking space across from the station.

How could she have been so obtuse as to expect she could simply walk into the police station, find Frank, and give him a piece of her mind? In the first place, they probably didn't *let* you see the chief just because you asked to. Especially if you looked like a vagrant. In the second place, he might very well refuse to see her. In the third place, she'd be making the same moronic mistake she'd made by going to the party, only worse.

77

Anybody who hadn't known who she was then surely knew now; that was probably part of the reason Frank hadn't called, although she'd given up trying to analyze that mystery. Not only wouldn't she be welcomed at the station; she'd be fortunate if they didn't have a bear pit waiting for her.

She got out of the car and ran into Carolyn's Diner, getting drenched. With fingers shaky from the wet chill and from the fury that still choked her, Ruth worked coins into the phone. To her surprise, the policeman who answered put her right through.

"Gordon."

His low, rich voice made her legs slacken. She held on to the shelf under the phone.

"Frank, this is Ruth Barrett," she said.

He was silent for a minute. Then he said coolly, "Hello, Ruthless."

"I need to talk to you about something very important. I'm across the street, in the diner. Will you come over?"

"Is this really necessary?"

"I promise you," she said, "if it wasn't a lot more than just necessary, there's no way I'd be standing here, dripping all over a pay phone—"

"I'll be there," he said.

She sat in a booth to wait. She would have liked to go into the rest room and try to create some order out of the mess that was her face and hair, but if he came in and didn't see her right away, he might leave.

A waitress came over, but Ruth's stomach was too jumpy for her to eat or drink anything. Anxiously she looked out the steamy window at the rain, still falling in steady lines.

Five minutes passed, then ten. Ruth's soggy sweats

were sticking to her skin and wetting the vinyl seat. She longed to go clean up, but she didn't dare. The waitress stopped again, and again she shook her head.

After twenty-five minutes she saw Frank walk out of the station and cross the street. He came inside, spotted her, and headed for the booth. He sat down, maneuvering to settle his big frame behind the table.

"So what's the big emergency?" he asked. "You can't be pregnant."

"Oh, God, Frank. You—" She stopped. However hard he worked at it, she had to prevent him from making her irrational. It would help nothing—not her, not Joan, not Chris. Certainly not the way her body went electric at the reality of having him right in front of her for the first time in two weeks.

She'd stick to the here and now. She had to.

"What took you so long?" she asked.

"Hey, babe, we have real work to do over there. We don't tap our toes for a living." His dark eyes were brooding. "Now, what's this about? It better be important."

"Oh, it definitely is that," Ruth said, "assuming you consider the attempted murder of a child important."

"Attempted murder? What the hell are you talking about?"

"I have a neighbor, Joan Lindsay," she said. "The one who was passing by when we, uh . . ." She felt her cheeks get hot, and rushed on. "This afternoon, her little boy was at the lake working on a school project when the storm started. He ran home through Mr. Zachariah's road—it would have taken him twice as long any other way, and the rain was ferocious—and the old psycho pulled his gun on that child! The poor kid was terrified. Of course, Joan called the police

79

immediately, but whoever she talked to implied that *Chris* was in the wrong."

She pushed her sticky hair back and leaned forward. "I've known Chris since he was a baby, and he's a darling boy. I'm as upset as if I were his mother. *That's* why I called. So I'm really sorry I disturbed you, Mr. Big Shot, but even you have to agree that this is a disgusting situation."

"I see," he said, sitting back and folding his arms, "that you have the whole thing all neatly packaged. No messy loose ends for me to have to worry about."

"I don't know what you mean," Ruth said. "Isn't it completely obvious that—"

"Simmer down, will you? The only thing that's obvious is that the desk sergeant wouldn't have responded to your neighbor in whatever way she didn't like without a reason."

"But all he—"

"Quiet! If you want me to deal with this, you'll proceed the way anybody else would have to. I'll ask you questions and you'll give me simple, factual answers. No histrionics. We'll do it *my* way, at *my* pace. Clear?"

Before Ruth could answer, the waitress was at the table again, summoned by Frank. Two policemen in uniform passed behind her. They waved to Frank and he nodded.

"I'll have a large Coke, Doreen," he said.

"No Sleepytime tea?" Ruth asked, loud enough for the other men to hear.

Frank ignored her. "What's the pie today?"

Ruth rolled her eyes.

"Coconut cream," the waitress said.

"A piece of that. A big piece. Anything for you?" he asked Ruth. "Carrot juice? Some raw liver?"

80

"No," Ruth said. "I'll just sharpen my teeth on this table."

The waitress left. Frank looked out the window and then back at Ruth. "Are you ready to answer my questions? Or do you want to play verbal stickball awhile longer? I can keep this up as long as you can, but a minute ago you were claiming to be concerned about your friend's kid."

"I wasn't *claiming*. I— Never mind." She pushed her hair behind her ears again. Her face was greasy and she felt clammy all over. Frank looked just the opposite, the picture of perfection in his uniform and leather jacket. Somehow the same rain that had rendered her a sodden mess in seconds had hardly touched him. A few drops glistened in his hair, but otherwise he could have walked across the street through an invisible tunnel. She could smell the leather—and Frank's warm and very masculine scent.

"What do you want to ask me?" she said.

"Number one," he said. "How old is this angelic child?"

"I thought these were going to be straight questions."

"That one was straighter than the facts you gave me, babe. Well?"

"Fourteen," she said tiredly.

"Uh-huh. Regular little toddler. How big is the kid?"

"He's very tall. He plays basketball. He—"

"I didn't ask for his résumé," Frank said. "What was the 'school project' he was working on at the lake?"

"Some of the kids were tidying up a picnic area."

"For?"

"What?"

81

"Why," he asked with heavy patience, "were they tidying it? For a Four-H outing? A senior citizens' picnic?"

"For a barbecue."

"When?"

"As soon as there's a decent day."

"So it wasn't any kind of official school deal."

"No," she said.

His Coke and pie came. The slice was the size of a football. He put away half of it in three bites before he spoke.

"Well," he said, "a very different picture is emerging here. Instead of a defenseless small child being terrorized as he returns home from a nature study class, we have a six-foot-plus young man hanging out and maybe raising a little hell by the lake. A young man who will happily contemplate freezing his buns off at a barbecue in March, but can't tolerate rain, choosing to trespass on private property known to be vigorously defended—and then crying to his mom that the old man scared him out of his wits." He pointed a long finger at her. "Are you beginning to have any inkling why the desk man responded to your friend's story with an impartial attitude?"

"Impartial? No," Ruth said definitely, shaking her head. "He practically accused Chris—"

"How exactly did he word his accusation?"

"I'm not sure. Joan didn't tell me. The man said they'd investigate."

"Uh-huh," Frank said, draining his glass. "And your friend concluded on that basis that the department would side with Zachariah."

"No. Not just that," she said. "There was more."

Frank went back to his pie. He finished it slowly.

Ruth watched him, free to do that since his attention was on his plate. She looked at the ridge of his jaw as it moved, the bristly skin she remembered the feel of so clearly from the night of the party.

She couldn't help it—she was dying to know what he thought about all that. He acted as though he'd forgotten they were ever anything but enemies. She wished she could just say, "Look, Frank, I'm curious. Why did you pursue me and take me out and kiss me, and then never call me again?" But she couldn't make the words come out.

Finally he said, "Let me guess what the rest of it was. I'm guessing your friend asked the officer whether he was accusing the boy of something, and he gave a noncommittal answer. I have a feeling that when your friend didn't hear 'No, ma'am, we'd never suspect your angel, that fiend will be arrested immediately,' she hit the ceiling. Am I anywhere near the truth?"

Ruth was silent.

Frank nodded. "No surprise. Look, Ruth, I understand why the lady is peeved, but she has to see our side. We're up to our armpits in teenage crime—"

"What! Chris is no criminal," she said hotly. "That's the trouble with the police—you all assume a child is a delinquent as soon as he gets out of training pants. You're much too rough on them."

"Will you listen a damn minute?" he said. "Whether you like it or not, it isn't paranoid in this day and age for an old man to figure he needs to defend himself against a fourteen-year-old big enough to play basketball. Now, I'm not assuming that'll turn out to be valid in this case. Maybe the kid is blameless. All the department can say is, we don't *know* till we check it out. That's the best I can tell you."

He put some money on the table and stood up. Ruth was sure he expected her to thank him. She'd choke first. She was going to just say good-bye and get out of here.

"Well—" she began.

"Don't mention it," he said, and left.

Frank hurried across the street. The rain hadn't let up, and he was anxious to get away from Ruth.

She hadn't seemed to want to stay too close to him either, but it wasn't how near or far she might be that worried him. It was his reaction to her: the way his eyes raked over her, searching out the contours under her bulky clothes that he'd known so briefly with his hands, the way his whole body leaped at her scent, the provocative fragrance that was like a part of her, the way he'd had to clasp his hands together under the table, not at all sure they wouldn't reach for her on their own. He wanted to get safely back inside the station, where everything there—the men, the whole atmosphere, everything—would remind him why this witch was fatal.

He glanced behind him and saw her taking a parking ticket from under the wiper of her Toyota. She wrenched open the car door and got in. He was tempted to go over, but he grabbed the door handle of the station.

He watched for another minute.

Later he'd have cause to relive that minute a hundred times. If, just before it, he'd continued on into the station and gone about his business, everything would have been fine. But instead he stood there, just long enough to hear the unmistakable sound of an engine with wet wires turning over but not catching. An engine that was going to flood if she kept leaning on the gas like that.

He went back across the street.

CHAPTER FIVE

"How can you forget to put money in a meter?" Frank asked as he drove to Ruth's apartment.

"What do you mean, how can I forget? People forget things. And I was distracted. I was very upset."

Handling the big Lincoln easily, Frank steered around a deep puddle and turned into Crestview.

"What do you want to do about the car?" he asked.

Ruth shrugged. "I'll call for a tow. There's nothing else I can do."

"Yes, there is. Just leave it. Tomorrow's supposed to be sunny. The car will dry out by the afternoon, and you can go down and get it," he said, carefully avoiding any suggestion of his participating.

"Won't I get ticketed again?"

"Not if they know the car's disabled. I'll call the desk from your place."

"Are you sure it'll be okay?" Ruth asked. "Isn't it likely I got the ticket to begin with because the man recognized me?"

"No. If he'd recognized you, you would have gotten a dozen tickets."

Frank parked and they went up to Ruth's apartment. She'd felt strange being in his car again, and she felt stranger still bringing him inside.

It had been clear that he'd rather eat matchbooks than drive her home. He probably thought this was the quickest way to get her off his turf. She hadn't wanted to accept the ride; the waves of hostility he emitted were so strong she could practically touch them, and for her part, Ruth was angrier at him than ever. The man just never seemed to run out of hideous ways to behave.

At the same time, she was experiencing something else—something that, when she'd agreed to call Frank, she'd hoped she wouldn't. She was as drawn to him as ever. He still exasperated her—and he still made her weak.

Well, she'd just have to cope. After everything that had happened, and not happened, between them, none of what she felt surprised her. In fact, she was proud that she could wear this cool air so well, pretend to him there was only dislike in her heart.

It would only take a minute, she thought as she unlocked her door, for him to call the desk. Then he'd be gone, and she could scream or throw things or howl at the moon if she wanted to.

Peaches came running over as soon as they were inside. She didn't always like to investigate guests, but she seemed to have a special interest in Frank. Ruth remembered the sight of his hand stroking the cat's belly the night of the party, and forced the picture out of her mind.

"You can use that phone," she said, pointing to her desk. She was starting to feel rattled.

Just stay calm for another minute, she told herself.

Frank dialed and spoke. He turned to Ruth. "Plate number?" he asked.

"What?" she said.

"Your license plate. What's the number?"

She knew her plate number fine, just as well as she knew her apartment number, her phone number, and the number of feet she had. But she was suddenly blank.

"I, um—I'll have to look. I don't— It's new," she babbled, lying.

He waited, phone in hand. Peaches jumped onto the desk and rubbed her head against his other hand. He massaged her back with long smooth strokes.

Ruth took her wallet out of her purse and flipped through the plastic windows looking for the registration receipt.

"Oh," she said, "I forgot. It's in the car."

"In the car," Frank repeated disgustedly. "I'll get back to you, Terry," he said, and hung up.

As he did, Ruth saw his jacket pull across his back and expose some of his white cotton shirt and the expanse of muscle under it. His pants fit flawlessly, not fussily tailored but just naturally right on his long legs.

To cover her lack of composure, she began to babble again. "I know you're not supposed to keep the registration receipt in the car," she said, going into the kitchen. "Everyone does, though, don't they?"

She started putting away dishes, moving from the sink to the cabinets as she talked. "Anyway, isn't it enough that they know what the car is and where it's parked? How many disabled white Toyotas can there be on Main Street in Lakeboro? Or can't you just check the plate on your way back to the station? Oh! I remember. It's nine-four-oh-five AXM."

"Lady," Frank said from the foyer, "you are one hell of a lot of trouble."

Something in his voice made her turn, a coffee mug

in each hand, to face him. He took a step toward her. His dark eyes were heavy with feeling, with emotions she couldn't decipher.

Her pulse galloping, she sought frantically for something to say, for more words to fill the cavernous space that had suddenly cracked open between them. But she was completely at a loss. She swallowed; it was the only movement she was capable of. She stood like a statue.

In two long strides Frank was in front of her. She gasped soundlessly, so certain he was going to touch her that she felt the sensation before it happened. But he dropped his hands and turned away.

"I'm getting out of here," he said.

"I think," Ruth said, finding her voice, "that's a good idea."

But he made no move toward the door. Ruth could see his neck and shoulder muscles tighten. She seemed to have forgotten to breathe.

Finally he turned back to her and pulled her to him in a grip that hurt.

"Damn you, Ruthless," he said. "Damn you to hell."

She felt the rough burn of his jaw against her face, and then her mouth was under his. He was kissing her with a desperate urgency, a heat that shocked her.

She no longer had to wonder if he'd forgotten their night together two weeks ago. She had no idea what he thought or felt, but on that point there was no doubt: he hadn't forgotten a thing.

He drew back just long enough to take the mugs out of her paralyzed hands and put them on the kitchen table. She watched him do it, her eyes following his every motion, knowing that in another instant his hands would be on her again and that it would be a

89

terrible mistake to let them stay there. But already she missed their exciting pressure, the hot promises they made all over her.

This time when he reached for her, it was to lift her, one arm under her back and the other supporting her knees. He turned toward the bedroom.

"Frank, no," Ruth said. She didn't want to—not this way, not with all her feelings turned upside down and out of control, not with him gripping her like that, half-passionate, half-furious. She kicked against his arm. "Put me down."

"Shut up," he said, and kissed her.

His lips were a great pressure. As he moved them on hers, she could feel none of the softness she remembered in her dreams. He forced her mouth open, and his tongue plunged hungrily.

Ruth was inflamed. While angry words fought to be voiced, her fingers moved to Frank's hair and clutched it. She was outraged that he'd refused to release her— but the rasp of his thorny skin against hers, the steamy male scent she inhaled as if she could never get enough of it . . . these were so much more immediate, battering at her misgivings.

When he felt her return the kiss he put her down in order to press her against his full length. His hands moved over her back, touching, gripping, sometimes with painful force. He squeezed her hip, and she cried out.

"Frank, stop," she said, her voice thick. She pushed at his chest. "Let go of me."

"Don't even bother to say it," he said.

"But I don't—"

"*Quiet.*" He took a handful of her hair and arched her head back. With his lips he followed the ridges of her throat, nipping as he went, not gently. His teeth on her tender flesh were an infuriating pleasure.

He moved down, past her collarbone, to where the zipper of her sweatshirt began. He held his mouth to the flushed softness that was the top of her breast while his strong hands pulled her lower body to his. His breath came fast and harsh as he held her there, and she gasped at the feeling.

He let go of her abruptly and yanked her zipper down. She tried to hold the shirt on, but he took it off and threw it aside. She had on the same pale-blue lace bra she'd worn when he pulled her out of the lake. As before, it was full and straining, and damp.

She tried to stop him from opening the bra's front clasp, but she didn't seem to be trying hard. He pushed her hands aside easily and pulled it off. He stepped back to look.

Ruth stood half-bare in front of his burning eyes, shaking. She was excruciatingly aware of his obsessive gaze.

"You might as well go ahead and look," she said between breaths, "because that's all you're going to do. I'm getting dressed." She bent to pick up her things.

He grasped her arm and brought her to her feet. She could feel his every finger pressing into her.

"Ruth," he said, "don't give me that. I'm going to do a lot more than look. I'm going to do everything."

"For the last time—"

"For the last time, close your mouth! You know it's going to happen. You can't stop it. I can't stop it. I'll have you on your bed or on the floor or up against the damn wall, but I'll have you now. You aren't really fighting me. You're fighting *it.*"

91

He picked her up again and carried her quickly into her room. He put her down next to the bed. She made a protesting sound, but her protests were growing less and less sincere. She was as powerless to stop the storm as he was.

As he'd known they would be, her breasts were round and smooth and swollen, inviting his hands, his mouth. But with an ache deep in his groin that was getting worse by the minute, he resisted. Hurrying, he took off her sweat pants, the heavy cotton sodden as the shirt had been, and the wisp of blue lace that was her panties.

Now she was naked, nearly his. She didn't seem to want to resist him at all anymore. He took off his jacket, then undid his belt and went to his shirt buttons, pulling roughly at them, as rushed as he'd been with her clothes. His eyes moved over her, lingering, now shifting, intent and ravenous as he undressed. The fragrance that came from her, the heavy perfume combined with her femaleness, was driving him crazy.

It was getting dark. Ruth saw Frank, the room, the bed, in a shadowy haze. Dreamlike, she saw him take off his shorts, and the response to his nudity coursed through her, an adrenaline-shot of wonder at his towering masculine presence.

He grabbed her around the waist and pushed her down on the bed.

"Ow! Frank!" she cried as if in pain, but it was passion in her voice. Her sensible, protective instinct was disappearing, obliterated by the fire in her blood. Her body—and her heart—were winning.

She felt his strong fingers everywhere at once, darts of flame on her arms and shoulders, on her stomach. Though she didn't mean for it to happen, her teeth came down on his shoulder. The love-bite was hard, and he drew in a sharp breath.

He opened her legs with a hand on each thigh and moved on top of her. His breathing was raw and uneven. She felt its hot rush on her face and breathed faster herself.

She was trembling hard. A mixture of desire and dread was taking her over, blanking out thought. Every physical fiber strained to join with the man above her in the ancient rhythm of surge and release, yet another part of her cried out to prevent it. She had a deep sense of something yearned for and yet very wrong, a mistake.

Frank grabbed her hands and held them pinned over her head in one of his as he entered her. Ruth felt his full force inside, and she gasped at her own burst of pleasure. The sound was muffled by his mouth. Quickly his motions became strong and rapid above her; he wouldn't, or couldn't, restrain himself.

Within moments Ruth was captured not only by Frank but by her own fierce need. She was a single force with him as they rocketed toward the heights. He said things in her ear; she didn't know what they were. She was lost, oblivious to everything but their motion.

A great rolling heat was carrying her, pushing her way up. The feeling was pure ecstasy—and agony. She'd never known such a powerful mix of emotions.

She sensed dimly that her face was wet, and that the wetness was tears, but she could obey nothing but the roar within her, the wonder that was Frank and what they had right now, this second, that no one had ever had before or would again. She met his body's ferocious strokes. There was desperation in the hunger that drove them, and when the peak came, it was that

93

much more exquisite and precious for their awareness of their short, turbulent past together, and their uncertain future.

They lay together for a long, still moment, each waiting for the other to speak first. Ruth had a feeling in the pit of her stomach that what had just happened had not solved any of their problems, that their problems had only just begun.

The room was too dark for her to see him well, but he didn't look different from when he'd come in. Only a sheen on his face, revealed by the pale light that came in around the window shades, gave a hint of the passionate lover he'd been minutes before.

"I'm sorry," he said then, his voice heavy and husky. "It shouldn't have happened. It won't happen again."

Ruth managed a weak nod. She wanted to say something, but nothing came. He had spelled it out: it shouldn't have happened.

She ought to be angry, she thought, but she wasn't. Maybe later. Now she was just hollow.

Five minutes later, he was dressed and gone. She heard her front door close with a final-sounding thud.

"Keep moving, keep moving," Ruth said, walking quickly around the floor with the class. "Find your pulse. Ready—count." She took her own pulse as she kept her eyes on the stopwatch. "Okay, stop. Your cool-down rate should be one-twenty or below. Write it down before you leave, please."

She turned off the tape player. "Good dancing, everyone. You're all looking great. Keep it up."

She took off her sweatband, dropped it in her duffel bag, and collected the pulse cards from the table in the big windowed room. Then she turned off the lights, put on her coat, and went out to the car.

She'd felt good in class, dancing with the easy, almost effortless rhythm she could achieve sometimes, but now she was drained again, as she'd been for the last couple of weeks.

She hated Frank Gordon for the way he'd run hot-cold-hot-cold with her feelings, but she was mad at herself too. She was partly to blame for letting him manipulate her heartstrings the way he had—and also for that insane afternoon in her apartment, so unreal that she sometimes thought it might have happened in her imagination.

It had taken a week for her to realize that some of her murderous feelings toward Frank were really a smokescreen for her own angry regret. She'd finally admitted that she could have stopped him if she'd honestly wanted to. But the insight hadn't made the cloud go away. Sometimes she could climb out of it, as she had this morning in her class—but mostly she just felt gray.

Her next class was at five; she had two hours to do her errands. She drove to Main Street, parked, and fed the meter. If she lived to be a hundred and ten, she'd never forget to put money in a parking meter again.

She dropped some pants and sweaters at the dry cleaner and cashed a check at the drive-in window of the bank. At the variety store she got plant food, hand lotion, and a new pillow. Her old one was in the trash; she'd aired it, sprayed it, and run it through the dryer, but she hadn't been able to get Frank's musky scent out of it.

She went to the hardware store for a fluorescent

bulb. Pete Pelland, its good-looking blond owner, grinned when she came to the counter.

"Hello, beautiful," he said. "How's my favorite athlete?"

"Okay, Pete. How are you?" She gave him the bulb and a twenty-dollar bill.

"Not as good as I could be."

"It must be an epidemic," she said.

"Excuse me?"

"Nothing. Just mumbling to myself."

He said, "Aren't you going to ask me what the trouble is?"

"No," she said.

"Too bad." He handed her the bulb in a bag. "I was all set to explain how you could make things better. Wine, nice music, some dancing—"

"Another time," she said.

"Promise?"

"No," she said, smiling.

She left the store with a lighter step. She'd never dream of going out with Pete—he changed women as often as he changed his underwear—but his flirting soothed her scraped ego. He always made her feel like a movie star, and right now, as she was feeling more like a termite, she needed that.

It was only four. There was no point in going home before her class, but she was hungry. She looked at Carolyn's, thought of a hot bran muffin, and started toward it. Then it occurred to her that Frank might be in there.

She turned and headed in the other direction. What other things could she do to kill an hour?

She stopped. Don't be a marshmallow, she told herself. You want a bran muffin? Go into Carolyn's and order it. If Frank is there, or if he comes in, ignore him. You're bound to run into him sometime. You can handle it.

She turned again and walked to Carolyn's and went in.

She remembered the smell as soon as she opened the door—a combination of steam heat, bacon, coffee, and frying oil. She'd smelled it for years; it was as familiar as the vinyl odor inside her car and the chlorine-cologne mixture of the fitness center. Now, of course, it just made her think of Frank—the raindrops in his hair, his white uniform shirt, the way she'd tried to state her case about Chris in a cool, assertive way with her hair sticking to her face, her soggy sweats hanging heavily on her, and her heart pounding furiously.

Well, what did she expect? It had been only two weeks ago. Right now everything said "Frank" to her, but she was working him out of her system bit by bit.

She glanced around quickly. No Frank—no police at all. Relieved, she sat in a booth and took off her coat.

The waitress Frank had called Doreen came over. "What can I get you?" she asked. Then, looking again, "Oh, hi."

"Hi," Ruth said.

"I like your hair a lot better this way."

"Uh, you do?"

"Much. It's fuller. Fluffier."

Just what she needed to dull the glow Pete Pelland had left. Doreen thought the rained-on mess had been her intentional hairstyle!

"So, what'll it be?" she asked.

"A toasted bran muffin, please, and orange juice."

The waitress left and Ruth looked out the window,

resting her chin on her hand. There was the police station, right across the street.

So what?

Her muffin and juice came, and she started on them.

It had been at the two-week point last time that she'd called Frank. She'd never have gone near him if it hadn't been for Joan and Chris, but the call had led to trouble, plenty of it. If she hadn't called, she'd probably be over him by now. Instead, she often found herself wakeful at two or three or four a.m., sometimes even all night. There would be a pain in her body, a physical embodiment of the hurt in her heart and her confused emotions.

Then the pictures would come rushing in. She'd remember the feel of him, all of him. She'd imagine him beside her, above her, in the bed again, his hands and mouth hurting and yet filling her with pleasure. And the finality in his voice: *"It won't happen again."*

Well, that went double for her. There would be no more calls. All she wanted was to wash this strange love-hate affair out of her life.

She found herself staring at the station. She looked quickly away, asked for the check, and took out her wallet. She paid and left.

"Any of the apple crumb pie left?" Frank asked.

"No," Doreen said. "I have blueberry and lemon meringue."

"I'll take that."

"Which? The lemon meringue? Your blond friend was in here, by the way."

"What?" Frank said. "Ruth? When?"

"Just left. You want the lemon meringue?"

He leaned toward the window and looked up and down the street. "How long ago?"

"Take it easy," she said. "You'll break your neck. It was about ten minutes." She adjusted her apron around her bony hips. "Which pie?"

He settled back in the booth. "Apple crumb."

The waitress sighed. "Earth calling Frank."

"Cut the comedy, Doreen. I'm not in the mood."

"Well, I can see that," she said. "Excuse me for living." She walked away.

"Wait," he said. "I'm sorry. I'm in a bad mood; I didn't mean to take it out on you." He smiled. "Friends?"

"Sure," she said. "But if that smile's the best you can do, you need more help than pie'll give you."

"Pie'll do fine," he said.

"Okay. Which one did you want?"

"I told you. Apple crumb."

"And I told you," she said with long-suffering patience, "that I'm out of apple crumb. Blueberry or lemon meringue."

"Either," he said, turning back to the window. "I don't care."

Doreen sighed again and went to the counter.

Ruth turned into Crestview. The sun was setting, but it wasn't that cold out. After the day's two classes she didn't feel like a run, but a short walk sounded appealing; she needed some fresh air.

The first thing she saw when she pulled into the lot behind her building was that a drainpipe had come loose and was hanging slightly away from the clapboard. The second thing she saw was Frank's Lincoln, parked with the motor running, with Frank at the wheel and someone next to him.

She hit the brake and the car stalled.

Frank saw her and shut off the engine. He got out, then his companion got out, and Ruth saw that it wasn't a person but a German shepherd.

She rolled down her window as she watched them walk over to her. Frank had his leather jacket and his sunglasses on. The jacket was open, showing the blindingly white shirt she remembered so well. His pants— She didn't want to look at his pants.

"Just getting home from the center?" he asked.

Ruth nodded, not sure she could talk.

"This is Judy."

She nodded again.

"Mind if I bring her in?"

"In?" Ruth repeated. "To my apartment, you mean?"

"Well," Frank said, "I wasn't going to put her in the Toyota."

"Sure, okay. Just let me park." Ruth's hand was trembling on the steering wheel. For a minute she had no idea what to do.

She sat staring at the gearbox, her heart racing. Frank was here, and he was coming upstairs. As soon as she parked her car. Which she was going to do if she could just remember how to start it.

She finally got going by making herself perform the starting procedure one step at a time: engage clutch, step on brake, turn key. The car bucked some as she drove into her space, but she got it there. She stepped out, locked the door, remembered her duffel, opened it, took the bag, and locked it again. She wasn't sure whether Frank could see her behaving like a dimwit, but when she glanced up to see how closely he was watching her, she saw that he didn't appear too together himself. He was as attractive as ever, but there were lines of fatigue around his eyes, and his mouth looked like it had forgotten how to smile.

"So," she said, walking over to him, "Judy is the police dog?"

"Yes," Frank said. "I'm taking care of her for a few days."

"Uh-huh," Ruth said.

There was a prickly silence.

He said, "I'd like to—"

She said, "What can I—"

There was silence again. Finally Frank said, "I'd like to come in and talk to you about something."

"Oh," she said. Of course; he'd already said he wanted to come in. Why was she standing out here like a parking attendant?

They went upstairs. "The dog won't hurt Peaches, will she?" Ruth asked.

"No, Judy loves cats. She never hurts them; she just plays rough."

Three guesses where she learned that, Ruth thought.

He said, "I guess you heard about Chris Lindsay. Phil Davids checked it all out, and there was no provocation or anything. Zachariah got a strong warning."

"Joan told me," Ruth said. She opened her door. Judy waited politely beside Frank, and went inside when he did. Peaches came running out of the bedroom, and screeched to a stop when she saw the dog.

Judy dipped her head to sniff the cat, and Peaches sniffed back.

"I guess that's what we're doing," Frank said.

101

"Sniffing. Or one of us is, anyway. I know why I'm here, but you don't."

She turned to look at him as coolly as possible. "Why don't you tell me, then?" she asked quietly.

It was a good thing her real feelings weren't reflected in her voice. She'd thought she'd never see him in her apartment again, and even now his presence seemed only half-real. Was he here because of Chris? Or did his sleepy eyes bespeak the same turmoil she felt?

"Let's sit down," Frank said, going into the living room.

Ruth followed, wishing he'd hurry up and speak his piece. If he drew this out one more minute, she wouldn't be able to keep up her tranquil pose.

He sat on the flowered couch and Ruth carefully took the chair farthest from him. He said, "The reason I came—" and there was a yowl from the bedroom. They both jumped up and hurried in. Judy had Peaches cornered. The dog was wagging her tail and panting happily, but the cat plainly didn't care to socialize.

Ruth picked Peaches up and shut her in the bathroom. They went back to the living room.

"What were you saying?" she prompted.

"I was saying that I want to—"

A terribly mournful sound arose. Ruth ground her teeth as they ran back into her room. Judy lay with her nose to the bathroom door, whimpering for her playmate.

"Frank," Ruth said, the last of her patience gone, "will you please tell me why you're here?"

He turned quickly at her tone. "It's a professional visit," he said.

"Your profession," she demanded, "or mine?"

"Yours. I came to—"

"I can't hear you. Could you please quiet her down?"

He crouched by the dog. "Judy, hush," he said. He sounded placating and not full of hope, like a parent watching a two-year-old have a tantrum; but when he began petting her in long, soothing strokes, her crying softened.

Ruth made herself look away.

"Anyway," Frank went on, "I still think this overweight stuff is a crock, but as you know if you read the paper, I'm pretty much alone on that. The whole damn town's on my back. Thanks to you."

Ruth said, "If you only want to browbeat me again—"

"No," he said firmly, "I don't. Believe it or not, I want your help."

She stared at him.

Judy was finally lying quietly. Frank rose to his feet. For the first time Ruth was struck fully by the impact of having him in her bedroom again. A sensual memory overwhelmed her suddenly, at once sweet and sad. Tears threatened; she took a deep breath to ward them off.

There he was, not five feet from her bed—the bed where he'd made love to her with a hunger that wasn't love, wasn't anything she could put a name to.

Frank clearly wasn't affected by being in here with her—or if he was, he hid it. His expression hadn't changed. They went back to the living room.

"Remember when I said I'd only gained five pounds since I was a kid," Frank asked her, "and you challenged me?"

"Did I? I don't remember saying anything."

"You didn't. You just looked at me as if I were trying to tell you I was from Pluto. Well, I finally weighed myself, and you were right—I'm fifteen pounds heavier. I couldn't believe it."

Ruth stayed tactfully silent.

"So," he said, "I've got to compromise a little." He leaned forward on the couch. "I don't think the department's fitness has a thing to do with the fact that muggings are on the increase. But I'm at a disadvantage arguing that point with a little extra poundage on. I figure if I can make a start, maybe get some of the others at least thinking about it, the pressure will die down."

"Then you want me to do what?" Ruth asked. "Suggest a diet? An exercise program?"

"Yeah," he said. "That."

"Which? Both?"

"Why not?"

Ruth sat back and studied him, frowning. Was he serious? Did he really expect that after everything that had happened, up to and including what had taken place in the very next room, they could now assume a working relationship?

"Let me ask you something," she said, picking her words carefully. "Do you think it's possible to establish a professional atmosphere and maintain it when there's been a, um, personal element to . . . ?"

"Yes," he said. "We're two intelligent adults. We're going to forget anything ever happened between us.

"I'm sorry about that afternoon. I regret that it happened at all," he went on with an oddly formal stiffness, "and for any hurt I caused you. Pain, I mean."

"I know what you mean," Ruth said, unnerved by

his pragmatic attitude toward the firestorm that haunted her.

"At least," he said, "we got it out of our systems."

He looked her straight in the eye then, and she couldn't look away. A current passed between them, a confounding thing she could not resist.

With an effort she broke the connection. To give herself some thinking room, she got up and went to the window.

Once again she was faced with a choice she hadn't expected. Should she say no, usher him out the door, and get on with the process of forgetting him? Maybe she should regard this as a second opportunity to do what she hadn't done two weeks ago—make the break permanent, before things went in yet another unpredictable direction.

Or did she stand a better chance of exorcising her leftover jumbled feelings about him once and for all if they *did* begin a professional relationship?

She didn't accept for a second that his interest in her was purely work-related at this point. *If all he wants is advice, why come to me? I'm not the only person in New Hampshire who knows about fitness and weight loss.* And if logic hadn't told her that, the look that had zinged between them moments before would have. People who only wanted to read calorie charts together didn't caress each other with their eyes. It was as plain as if he carried a picket sign: he cared for her. He was attracted to her. Whatever other feelings he had, those were clearly there.

Probably Frank was experiencing something like what she was—a mishmash of unresolved emotions he wished he could straighten out. Maybe that was what he hoped to do by getting together with her, besides working on his fitness. In any case, he *did* seem sure that a detached relationship was what he wanted, and that he'd have no trouble maintaining it.

She didn't know whether she'd like the arrangement Frank was proposing, but the alternative was what she'd *been* doing: sleeping badly, laughing little, coming out of her zombie state only to lead her classes, constantly pushing away burning scraps of memory that fought hard for her attention. This way couldn't be any worse.

If he can keep his distance, so can I.

"All right," she said from the window. She turned to him. "I'll do it."

"Good," he said matter-of-factly. He might have been talking to someone about supplying batteries for his two-way radio. "What do you suggest?"

"Let me think about it," Ruth said. She'd made all the decisions she was capable of for the moment. The moment being the next ten years.

"Well, how much thinking will you have to do?"

"I need a little time," she said. "I can't just tell you to eat two radishes and call me in the morning. I'll work out a plan and call you. Okay?"

He got up. She was dazzled all over again when he stood, impressed by his larger-than-life proportions, his long and muscular legs, the thighs hard under the dark pants.

If she was going to stop thinking of him like that, she'd better start now. She looked away, wishing he'd take his chaperon and go. Or she might start hoping to hear words he wasn't going to say, to experience things they weren't going to do. She might start imagining he'd stop at the door and turn this whole business around.

The obedient dog heard Frank get up, and met him in the foyer. Ruth opened the door.

"Oh," he said. "Something important I forgot to say."

"Yes?" Ruth asked. Her pulse sped up and her fingers felt cold suddenly.

"You have a piece of drainpipe down. Better get it fixed before another storm makes it worse," he said as he walked out the door.

CHAPTER SIX

"I'd better get my ears checked," Phil Davids said. "You wouldn't believe what that sounded like. I said to you, 'Hey, Frank, let's get a couple of cold ones tonight,' and I could have sworn you said, 'I can't—I'm going to a diet group meeting.'"

"That's what I said, Phil," Frank told him. He got up from his desk and opened the window. It was still cold out, but it was sunny, and the office was stuffy.

"You're serious?" Phil said. "A *diet* group?"

"That's right."

"One of those places where they weigh you and tell you what to eat? You're really doing that?"

"You know, Phil," Frank said, "you seem to think that if you ask me the question enough times, you'll get a different answer."

"Well, hell. You kind of knocked me over." Phil sat down in a leather chair by the desk. "How come? I thought you liked your weight fine the way it is."

"I do," Frank said.

"And even if you don't, why do you need this group thing? Can't you just go on a diet yourself if you . . . what did you say?"

"I said I am satisfied with my weight."

"That's what I thought," Phil said. "So? Why go to a diet group?"

Frank leaned back in his big wooden swivel chair. His shoulders pushed at the shirt fabric. "Why do you think, Phil?" he asked deliberately.

The other man studied him for a minute. "Ohhh," he said finally. "Throw the folks a bone."

"You got it."

Phil chuckled. "Want me to call the *Banner?*"

"No," Frank said. "I don't want a sideshow. They'll find out fast enough anyway. When the Lakeboro police chief whose gut gets more space in the paper than *Doonesbury* waltzes into Pounds Off and says 'Where do I sign?' they're bound to hear a little something."

"You won't be looking for company on this, though, will you?" Phil asked, his thick brows drawing together.

"What do you mean?" Frank asked sharply.

"I don't have to go with you, do I?"

"You? No, buddy."

"I'll always help you out, you know that," Phil said. "But I've spent a lot of years building this." He patted his big stomach. He was much shorter than Frank, and his excess weight was obvious. "It would be like hacking away at the Rock of Gibraltar."

"Well, a police officer's weight is his business," Frank said. "I'd never make any of you diet."

"Right on," Phil said. "You keep telling those loudmouths where to go."

Frank drove into the YMCA lot. He didn't see Ruth's Toyota. He parked and settled back to wait.

He didn't like the way he was looking forward to seeing her again—but at least he was in better shape

109

than before he had gone to her place to ask for her help. Up until then he'd been unfit to be near. Things had just kept piling up on him until he was a tinderbox of tension—the constant hassles over the weight issue, more muggings, and then, on top of everything, that disastrous afternoon with Ruth.

He'd been enraged at himself for not being able to resist her, and for thinking that going to bed with her would get her out of his system. Since that afternoon, she'd been on his mind even more than before, invading his routine, leaving him totally unsettled and unable to give his all to the department. It was an impossible mess.

That was why he'd decided to go to her. He couldn't predict what would happen between them. All he knew was what he couldn't do, and that was not see Ruth Barrett. He hadn't really lied about wanting only a professional relationship; he did want that, or his head did, anyway. As for the rest of him, he wasn't wagering any guesses.

And the other factor, the publicity value of the diet effort, was important too. There was a good shot it'd reduce the flak. As for the exercise—it would give him a reason to be with her still more. And finally, while he knew five or fifteen pounds more or less made no difference in his ability to do his job, he *had* been shocked that it was fifteen. He might look better with an inch off the middle.

He checked his dashboard clock: six twenty-five. It was nearly dark. Close-set headlights beamed across the pavement; Ruth was here. He noticed that there were plenty of other cars coming in, too, which meant that it was probably a big group.

Good, he thought. Easier to lose yourself.

He got out of the car and went to the Toyota just as Ruth was stepping out. Her parka hood was down, and her yellow hair gleamed in the white light of the lot.

"Have you been waiting long?" she asked.

He caught a whiff of her scent and turned his face away. He jammed his hands in his pockets.

"Not long," he said. He watched her lock the car. "You told your neighbor we'd be here?"

"Yes."

"Was she surprised?"

Ruth said, "The only time I've seen her more surprised was when Hurricane Gloria blew all her windows in."

"Hell. She won't single me out or anything, will she?"

"Absolutely not. She's very sensitive. She wouldn't do that with anybody," Ruth said. "Joan's been running diet groups for as long as I've known her, and that's, oh, twelve years. She'd never embarrass anyone."

They went inside and down to the large well-lighted basement room where Pounds Off met every Thursday. About forty people were already seated in the rows of folding chairs. Ruth saw Joan at the front, laying materials out on a table for her lecture. She looked striking in a scarlet knit dress that set off her black hair. A balance scale stood behind her, and a woman Ruth knew as Joan's assistant was weighing the group members.

"I'm not doing that," Frank said, taking a seat near the back and folding his arms.

Ruth sat next to him. She started to argue, but thought better of it. There would probably be a lot of contention once he got moving with his diet and exercise, and things would go more smoothly if she gave in on some issues.

"We'll talk to Joan after the meeting," she said. "I'm sure she can arrange to do your weight in private."

"I can do my own weight on my own scale," he said with finality.

Ruth gave up.

The weighing was over and everyone took seats. Joan began the meeting with a pep talk about spring and how nice they'd all look in their warm-weather outfits.

Next to Ruth, Frank was fidgeting like a third-grader. "Damn it," he said, "you told me this was a coed group."

Ruth looked around. He was right; the room was all women.

She said, "I know there are several men in the group. I made sure of it."

"Well, where the hell are they? Hiding under the chairs?"

"I guess they're just not here tonight. People miss meetings."

Frank made a sound of disgust and slid lower in his seat.

Joan finished her opening talk and invited the members to contribute. Several hands went up. She called on a plump woman of about sixty with fuzzy gray hair.

"Looks like she has a squirrel on her head," Frank said quietly to Ruth.

The woman described a recipe she'd developed for low-calorie "spaghetti." She heated bean sprouts in a nonstick pan, she said, and made a "sauce" out of boiled-down tomato juice.

"It tastes just like the real thing," she said proudly.

"When my family sits at the table and smells that delicious Italian aroma, why, they can't tell the difference. I call it 'Lillian's Mock Pasta Italienne Supreme.'"

The other members clapped enthusiastically and began suggesting additions. When someone mentioned grated carrots and a collective "ooh" swept the room, Frank's jaw dropped.

"That," he said with awe, "is truly sickening."

"Shh," Ruth said. "Give it a chance."

"Are you kidding? They'll be putting salamanders in this recipe in a minute."

"I don't mean the recipe. I mean the whole meeting. Why don't you just relax and listen?"

"There's nothing worth listening to!" he whispered loudly. Several women turned to look. When they saw that the troublemaker was a huge man sitting off alone with a woman who clearly didn't need to be there, they stared harder. Some tapped others and pointed.

"Damn it to hell," Frank muttered, trying to slide even lower in his chair. Ruth's face burned. This wasn't at all how she'd envisioned things.

"Look," she said, "I know this part is boring, but try to be patient. I think Joan just likes to start off informally before she gets into the serious aspects of the meeting."

As soon as Joan introduced the next activity there were shouts of approval and applause. Ruth had been too occupied with Frank to hear what it was, but she was pleased to see all the attention focus on the front of the room again.

A woman walked up to Joan's table. Joan held her arm while she climbed onto it. She needed help so she wouldn't trip on the pants she wore, which flapped voluminously around her; they were twice as big as she was.

"Two years ago I was wearing these," she said triumphantly, and the group cheered. She held the waistband out, then turned to show the back. She lost her hold for a moment, revealing a knee-length pink panty girdle.

Frank covered his eyes and moaned.

A slimmer woman came to the table and was helped up. The room exploded in laughter as she climbed into the pants too.

Ruth glanced at Frank. He looked truly pained. She grabbed his arm, determined to help him stick this out.

"I'm sorry," she said. "I'm embarrassed too. But I'm sure most meetings are more dignified than this. Please give it time. You'll be glad you did—Pounds Off's results are the best."

He looked at her hand. She looked at it too, and yanked it away.

What he really wanted right now was to stand up, head quickly for the Exit sign behind him, and get very far away from here very fast. He'd been all set to do it, and he would have—if the sexily scented lady next to him had kept quiet, or said something that just ticked him off more. But she'd caught him off guard with her whispered pleas, her warm breath an intimate tickle in his ear. And what had really done it was her hand, the slim fingers surprisingly tight on his forearm. It had propelled him right back to that scene in her bedroom, the one he'd told her had gotten this stuff out of their systems. Her grip had been tight then too, her delicate but strong hands all over him, her legs . . .

Ruth's hand burned, really burned. She clutched it

with the other one, her face turned away so Frank wouldn't see how her carefully neutral expression had slipped.

She should never have touched him. The knots of muscle under his sleeve had felt painfully familiar. She wouldn't make that mistake again.

She looked at her watch. It seemed as if they'd been there in the basement room for hours; she was astonished that only twenty minutes had passed. She knew from her long friendship with Joan that the meetings were usually more serious than this, but Frank would never come back if he gave up now.

She glanced covertly at him. He looked as though he were trying to be patient. She might be misjudging him. After all, the whole fitness effort had been his idea; maybe in spite of his protests he was really getting used to being at the meeting.

Probably everything would be fine. She relaxed a bit.

Joan's assistant pushed the scale to the front of the room, putting it where everyone could see it. Ruth wondered what this part of the meeting was.

Joan said, "Ladies, let's settle down. It's great to have fun—that's a vital part of weight loss, as we've learned—but now it's time to get serious."

Thank heaven, Ruth thought. She felt Frank relax a little next to her. Now that the nonsense was over, there ought to be valuable information. Maybe Frank would learn some tips that would get him started.

"This group," Joan said, "is about to be in on the making of history. Lakeboro history, that is."

Ruth frowned.

"Many of you have read in the *Banner* that our police are being criticized because of their weight. Well, tonight, right here at Pounds Off, Chief Frank Gordon is going to set an example for his department by making his first weigh-in in front of all of—"

Ruth didn't hear any more. Three chairs went crashing to the floor as Frank jumped up and hurried from the room. She ran after him, but he got a head start while she was shoving the chairs aside, and by the time she reached the lot his Lincoln was racing down the street.

"Ruth, my God!" Joan said behind her. "Wasn't that what he wanted?"

Ruth turned stricken eyes to her. "I . . . what?"

"I think I made an awful mistake," Joan said. "I just assumed—I mean, with the flap in the paper and everything—well, I figured Frank would want to make a big thing out of his coming here. To show that he was trying. I thought I could do him a favor. He was so nice to help with Chris, I wanted . . . Ruth? You look terrible. What have I done? I'm so sorry." She shivered in the wind.

Ruth rubbed her eyes and looked dismally back at the street. "It's not your fault," she said. "I should have explained that he wanted to stay in the background. But since you're always so careful not to call attention to people—"

"I know. I see now. What a mess. How can I fix this?" She put her hands in her dress pockets. "I have to get back inside, but let me know if there's anything I can do."

Ruth started the car. She had to find Frank, to explain that she'd been taken by surprise too. She'd feel awful if he thought he'd been set up.

She went to his building. She didn't see his car, but

116

she went in and rang the bell anyway. There was no answer.

Now what? Could he have gone to the police station? She thought he worked regular daytime hours, but who knew with policemen? It wasn't as if the place closed at the end of the day.

She drove into town. Main Street was as deserted as it always was on a week night, except for the police station, the movie house—and Carolyn's. There was the Lincoln, in front of the diner. She parked next to it and went in.

He was sitting in a booth with an enormous Coke in front of him. She slid in.

"I'm sorry," she said quickly. "Horribly sorry. That was a complete misunderstanding. Joan assumed you wanted publicity, and I never thought to warn her that you didn't." She took a quick breath and hurried on. "Do you believe me? I hope so, because all I want is to keep our agreement and help you start a fitness routine. I had no idea she was planning to—"

"Relax," he said. "You'll hyperventilate."

"I only—"

He reached across the table, held her head, and put his hand over her mouth.

"Well, this is cute," Doreen said, setting a two-inch-thick roast beef sandwich in front of Frank. "It isn't enough that we have crime in the streets—a girl isn't safe in here, either."

Frank took his hands away. "Not funny, Doreen."

"Muggings aren't funny either, Frank, but we had another one tonight. These kids are getting unstoppable."

Frank looked at her. "How do you know about the mugging? It won't be in the paper till tomorrow."

She gestured toward the kitchen with a toss of her frosted head. "Scanner."

Frank snorted. "Damn things. Just what we need, our radio frequency on display to anyone with a battery. You might as well put on a hat and join the department, Doreen, since you know so much."

The waitress's eyes blazed. "Gee, Frank," she said, "do you think I'm fat enough?"

He jumped up, his face hard, but Doreen went into the kitchen and he slowly sat down.

"You're really getting it from all sides, aren't you?" Ruth said.

He glared at her.

"Well," she said uncomfortably. "Anyway. I, uh . . . I'm glad you believe me. You do, don't you?"

"Yes," he said. He sighed and sat back. "It wasn't your style."

She wasn't sure how to take that. She decided to let it pass. "I hope you won't let this experience discourage you," she said. "Listen, there's a diet group around here that's all men. I've heard about it. Let me see what I can find out."

"I don't know, Ruth," he said wearily. "This group stuff isn't for me. No way am I going to walk into anything again like that deal tonight. I'd rather get the weight off surgically."

Doreen was passing by. "I'll perform the surgery," she said sweetly.

"If it was all men—" Ruth began.

He shook his head. "Too much trouble."

"But," she said, "this was your idea. You came to me."

"Well, hell, Ruth, I'm very busy." He finished his

118

sandwich. "I can't be waltzing to meetings all the time."

"All what time? It would only be once a week. You know, you don't seem very committed to this. When you came to see me, I thought you were sincere."

"I am. I just don't want to make a career out of losing weight."

Ruth looked at him. Her light eyes were narrowed. "I'm getting the feeling," she said, "that you have an ulterior motive. That you aren't as interested in fitness as you are in *looking* interested. Maybe Joan was right. You don't want a brass band, exactly, but you're pretty conscious of public relations."

"Of course I'm—"

"Want anything, hon?" Doreen said. "Bran muffin?"

"No, thank you. What I meant, Frank, was—"

He said, "Any police chief has to—"

"How about you, Frank?" Doreen asked. "Want anything else?"

He turned to her. "Yes, Doreen. I want you to stop bugging me. Give me the check, and don't say another word. I'll pay it and leave you a nice tip, if you'll just get out of my face."

"You can take your nice tip," she said, "and—"

"Doreen!" someone yelled from the counter. "Your burgers are ready."

With a last malevolent glare, she walked away.

"Don't mind her," Frank said. "She always gets upset when there's a mugging. She's afraid she'll be next."

"She won't be," Ruth said. "And stop changing the subject. You really *did* start this weight-loss project just to pacify people, didn't you?"

"No, not *just* for that. I admit it wouldn't be as important if I wasn't on the line—but don't give me any bull. I made no bones about that in the first place."

"You seemed a lot more serious than you do now," Ruth said. She was getting angry. She'd tried in good faith to help him, as he'd asked, but he appeared to be using her. "It looks as if all you want is to quiet the people who say the police are too heavy to chase teenage criminals. Well, you know what?" She stood up. "I'm not interested in helping you do either one of those things. I won't help you put on a show for your critics—and I won't help you harass kids any more than you already do!" She ran outside.

She'd just reached the car when Frank caught up with her.

"Hold on," he said. He took her car keys out of her hand and put them in his jacket pocket. "You're not going anywhere until I've had my say."

"*Your* say!" Ruth yelled. "*I'm* the one—"

"Yes, you are the one!" Frank shouted. "The one who single-handedly started this whole miserable mess! Do you have any idea what kind of an avalanche I'm sitting at the bottom of because of you?" He began pacing the empty street, back and forth. "Remember what Doreen said in there, how she busted my chops? Well, babe, multiply that by about fifty, and you'll have a day in the life of Frank Gordon. And Doreen's a *buddy*. Try to imagine what I hear from the ones who aren't my friends. I get hate mail, for God's sake! Phone calls—"

"And all this is my fault? No, Frank," Ruth said. She was shaking at the injustice of his blaming her for everything that was happening to him. "If you and your men weren't too heavy and complacent to do your jobs the way you—"

"Don't you dare!" he yelled. He stood facing her, his hands on his hips, towering, looming. "Don't tell me about my job! It isn't your damn business, and it never was!"

"Oh, yes, it is," she said. "It is when I see the police bully innocent kids just to look like they're on top of the mugging problem."

"Bully innocent kids!" Frank repeated at the top of his lungs. "Where in hell did you *ever* get an idea like that?"

"I hear about it all the time! I know a lot of kids, Frank—I'm more on their wavelength than you are. They tell me about being stopped in their cars, questioned at school."

He slammed his fist into his palm. "That's garbage. Bullying!" he scoffed. "No kid in Lakeboro gets our attention without a reason. You're so damn gullible!"

A pigeon alighted on the sidewalk near them. "Yes!" Ruth shouted, and it took off. She'd never been so mad. Even her voice was shaking now. To hide it, she yelled louder. "Yes, I am gullible! So gullible that I got the fright of my life when big Frank Gordon decided to try some of his bullying on me!"

"What the hell are you yapping about now?"

"Oh, please! Don't tell me you forgot! You let that awful old man Zachariah scare the life out of me, and you enjoyed it!"

"Hang it up!" he yelled. He started pacing again, his fury evident in each thunderous step. "Are you still holding on to that? It's over!"

"It's not over!" Ruth screamed. She wanted to sock him. He was totally blind to any view but his own. "You don't get over that sort of experience just like that! And because you didn't do enough, he pulled the same deranged trick on a child! And you accuse me of 'holding on' to this, as if I were still blaming you for stepping on my foot."

"You are hanging on to it. You're keeping it alive," he accused, "so you can have something to blame me for instead of blaming yourself—for all you've done to hurt me! For turning my job and my life upside down!" He screamed the last words.

"Frank, listen to yourself!" Her throat hurt. The movie house had just opened for the evening show; people going in were glancing across the street at them. "You insist I shouldn't be mad—but it's perfectly fine for *you* to keep berating *me* about the *Banner* article!"

"What? Where do you get your damn nerve? You can't compare—"

"Oh, I certainly can," she said. "As far as motive goes, what you did was worse! You say I hurt you—but if I did, it was completely unintentional. There's a dangerous situation in Lakeboro, and I was trying to do something to help. What I told the *Banner* had to be said, for the good of the town. It wasn't a personal attack against you!"

"You bet your sweats it was personal! You attacked the department. I *run* the department!"

"But—"

"I'm not finished. Thanks to you, every local yokel is running around complaining that the town isn't protected. It's my job to protect the town! That's as personal as it gets!"

"But I told you," Ruth said, "it wasn't intentional! What you did to me was on purpose. You were waiting for a chance to get back at me. You admitted you were!"

"Well, damn if you didn't deserve it!" he snapped.

The door of the diner opened and Doreen came out in her coat.

"Ugh, what a day," she said. "You two might want to keep it down to just a holler. You've got a front-row audience."

Frank and Ruth looked where she pointed. Several faces were crowded at the diner window.

"Oh, no," Ruth said. She covered her face with her hands.

"Don't sweat it, hon," Doreen told her, patting her arm. "This gorilla can get a person going. Like he did to me tonight." She turned to Frank. "Sorry."

"Yeah. Me too," he said.

Doreen walked away.

"Did I hear right?" Frank asked Ruth. "Were you actually admitting you hurt me?"

"Well—yes, I guess I admit that," Ruth said. "But not on purpose. That's a big difference." She looked at the diner window. The watchers were still there, clearly hoping for some more good stuff. She'd be damned if she'd oblige them.

"Then you understand that you got me in the worst trouble of my career by shooting off your mouth—"

"Oh, stop!" she said in a fierce whisper. "I was reasonable enough to admit I caused you harm. I don't see *you* climbing off your gunboat to take any blame. You're too busy screaming at me."

"You don't want much, do you?"

"No, Frank, I don't. It isn't wanting a lot to expect you to acknowledge you were at least a bit wrong in what you did to me!"

"What makes you think I don't?" he yelled. Ruth glanced at the window and he turned and looked himself. He lowered his voice. "I said you deserved it. I didn't say it wasn't a low thing to do."

"Oh," she said.

She let out her breath. She felt her body untense a little, like an overinflated balloon losing its extra air.

Something similar seemed to be happening to Frank. He still loomed over her, big as ever, but there was nothing threatening in his stance.

She felt his eyes on her and met them. Minutes ago they'd flamed with wrath, but now they were softer, not exactly friendly but not hostile either.

Ruth was beginning to see that what he'd been going through was a lot more serious than she'd thought. She certainly hadn't meant to hurt him—she hadn't even known him when she gave the interview, and everything she'd said in it was valid. But she couldn't argue with his complaint that, if it weren't for her, he'd be under a lot less fire.

She'd never accept that she deserved the gun trick—but she could understand why Frank would think so.

Someone came out of the diner, and she looked at the window. People were still watching. She stuck out her tongue.

Frank laughed. "Could be," he said, folding his arms and leaning against his car, "we ought to think about one more new start."

"On a diet routine, you mean?" she asked.

"On us," he said. "Just friends—arm's length. See what happens."

She felt a lot more air leave the balloon. "You think that would work?"

He shrugged. "Do you?"

"I don't know. Maybe."

He stood up. "Maybe's good enough. Maybe's all we've got."

He held out his hand to her. She gripped it. She felt something scratchy and realized he hadn't been offering his hand—he'd been giving back her keys. She turned away and bent to unlock her car door so he wouldn't see her blush.

He tapped her shoulder and she reluctantly turned back to him. He held out his hand again. She looked at it, then at his face, and took it.

He shook it formally, gave her a hint of a grin, and left.

CHAPTER SEVEN

"Ruthless," Frank said between breaths, "I was . . . right the first . . . time. You're . . . impossible. I hate this."

"It gets easier," Ruth said. "You can't develop good wind if you don't get out of breath."

He was silent except for his hoarse breathing. His rubber soles thumped along the lake track.

"Talk," she prompted him. "You have to keep the conversation going."

"Bull. It's enough that . . . I keep my . . . feet going. How can you . . . chatter away like that?"

She shrugged without breaking stride. "I'm used to it. You will be too, sooner than you think. Be patient. You've only been running for three weeks, and you don't do it every day."

He groaned.

"Noises don't count. Speak in sentences."

"Okay. Here's one. Time . . . for a rest."

"Not yet. Another quarter mile."

He groaned again.

"You can do it. Distract yourself. Don't concentrate on how uncomfortable you are. Ignore that."

"Like ignoring . . . a bullet in your knee."

"Look over there, where the shore hooks in. A

whole formation of ducks. They're interesting to watch. I love ducks."

"So do . . . I. Roasted, with . . . orange sauce."

Ruth's laugh floated out over the water. They continued on down the track. It curved as the lake did, looping along the bank, dipping toward or away from the shoreline every so often to skirt the trees and bushes.

There were no more ice chunks on the lake, and the fresh green smell of spring was unmistakable. The bone-gnawing wind off the water was subsiding into the steady breeze that whipped the lake in April, the precursor to summer's whisper.

Watching the new season come in was especially nice this year because a similar process was occurring in Ruth's life. Something new and sweet was beginning. Like spring, it rose from the ravages of a harsh beginning. And like spring, it was growing slowly, so slowly, but heavy with promise.

She realized she hadn't been reminding Frank to talk. "Hey," she said. "I gave you a little vacation."

"I was wondering when . . . you'd notice. All right. That's enough. I've . . . had it."

"Okay," Ruth said, slowing. "We'll walk back to the car, and that should be enough of a cool-down."

The Lincoln was warm inside from the sun. Ruth sank down with pleasure on the soft seat.

"What a gorgeous day," she said. "I wish I didn't have to go inside now."

"What time is your class?" Frank asked, starting the car.

"Four. I'll just have time to change and get over there." She wiped her face with both hands. "A shower would be nice, but I'll be taking one after class anyway. I wouldn't want your aunt to think I'm not a lady."

"She's anxious to meet you," Frank said.

"I'm looking forward to it, too. I'm a little nervous, though."

"Nervous? Why?"

"Well," Ruth said, "she's kind of intimidating, isn't she? The way you talk about her, she seems . . . I don't know, exacting."

"I wouldn't call Aunt Joyce intimidating. She commands respect, I guess you'd say. And I do think highly of her. She practically raised me."

Frank stopped in front of Ruth's building. "Have a good class," he said. "I'll pick you up at quarter to seven." He took her hand and brought it to his mouth. He kissed the tips of her fingers. Then he pulled on her hand to bring all of her closer, and kissed her gently.

As always when they kissed or touched each other, Ruth wished for more—for a taste of the searing dream they'd shared that afternoon that seemed years ago. As the weeks wore on, the memory evolved in her mind from being one of fleeting passion to being one of real love. She knew it was wishful thinking, but she let herself fantasize anyway. The fantasies would have to be enough.

Frank had kept his vow that their new start would be slow and easy, and Ruth was glad. Well, mostly glad. Everything about their relationship, right up to their fight outside Carolyn's, had been so rushed and tempestuous, it was a delicious luxury to get acquainted in all the ways they'd never had a chance to. But that afternoon haunted her, made her tremble as she remembered.

Frank pulled away reluctantly. He ran a hand down her arm and abruptly turned on the radio, as if trying to distract himself.

Ruth said, "Do you mind if—" Her voice was foggy. She cleared her throat. "Can I meet you at the restaurant at seven instead? I can use the extra few minutes."

"Sure," Frank said. "I made a reservation at Bradello's. You can meet us there."

He kissed her fingers a last time, and she went up to change.

The parking lot was surprisingly full, even for a Saturday night. People must want to get out more now that spring is around the corner, Ruth thought as she backed into a space on the street.

She wasn't thrilled with Frank's choice. She loved Italian food and indulged in it occasionally, but Bradello's cuisine was particularly caloric. It wasn't a great place for Frank to be eating, either. He had enough trouble staying sensible in more health-conscious restaurants—even in places specializing in fish and chicken, he always managed to end up with a huge steak in front of him.

But she hadn't wanted to suggest they eat somewhere else. She was trying hard to avoid arguments; he seemed to be doing the same. She supposed it was natural that, after their tense beginning, they were making an effort to be scrupulously sensitive.

And there would have been no point in arguing about the restaurant anyway. Frank just wasn't going to be as serious about his diet and running as she thought he ought to be. He did stick to a minimum regimen, but he'd made it plain that that was it.

She went inside and looked for Frank and his aunt.

She felt a tap on her shoulder, and she turned. There he was with a very tall and fine-boned woman holding his arm. She had Frank's large, definite features, but her brown hair, parted in the middle and caught back in a twist, was brushed with gray. She wore a charcoal gray cashmere designer suit which made Ruth feel self-conscious about her casual turtle-green sweater dress.

Frank made introductions; he seemed a little ill at ease. They were shown to a comfortable table near a fireplace. The smell of woodsmoke was pleasant in the room.

"It's lovely in here," Ruth said to break the silence.

"Are you too warm, Aunt Joyce?" Frank asked.

"No, dear," she said. "I always enjoy a fire. What about you, Miss Barrett? Do you like a wood fire?"

"Please, call me Ruth. Yes, I love them. Especially since I don't have a fireplace myself."

"This restaurant seems quite popular," Aunt Joyce commented, looking regally around the room. "At such an early hour, too. I have to admit, I do miss the more civilized dinnertimes of the old days. When Frank was growing up, we never sat down to the evening meal before eight o'clock. You haven't kept to those customs, Frank."

"Uh, no, Aunt Joyce. I get hungry," Frank said sheepishly.

"Indeed," the woman said, eyeing his stomach.

His mouth tightened, but he didn't say anything.

A waiter handed them menus. "Would you like to order drinks?" he asked, taking out his pad.

"A glass of seltzer water, please," Aunt Joyce said, "with a lemon slice but no ice."

The waiter looked at Ruth. She said, "I'd like a very dry—"

"—napkin," Frank said. "Hers is wet. Some water got spilled on it. And she'll have a Tab to drink."

Ruth turned to Frank, her mouth open. He didn't look at her.

"Ginger ale for me," he told the waiter.

Ruth's mouth opened wider. Frank shot her a warning look and she closed it.

The waiter left and they opened their menus. Well, Ruth thought, so much for the lady Frank "wouldn't call intimidating." Apparently she was a teetotaler and wanted others to be too. It was funny, actually; Ruth wouldn't have thought there was a force on the planet that could keep Frank from having his usual beer.

Frank suggested several veal and chicken dishes for his aunt. He pointed out two seafood selections to Ruth. She was chagrined but not surprised when he ordered lasagna for himself.

Conversation went more easily after that. Frank got his aunt chatting about some antiques she'd recently bought. Ruth knew nothing about the topic, but he did, and he directed the talk so she could participate.

Aunt Joyce asked Ruth about her work, and she described her job at the fitness center and the tasks involved in maintaining her apartment building.

"Excellent," the woman said. "Very independent and courageous of you. You're clearly a most capable young woman, Ruth. My, this was superb. They do a fine job with veal here."

Frank finished the last of his lasagna. "If you ladies don't mind," he said, "I'll be back in a minute."

He stood up. Ruth had never seen him in a suit before, and though she knew she ought to keep her

131

eyes demurely on her plate, or the wall, or anywhere but on Frank, she couldn't resist taking a minute to admire him. His jacket fit perfectly across his steamship-wide shoulders, and as he turned to move his chair, it fell open to show the rugged chest she remembered so well. He had no extra weight on his hips, and they tapered in a lean curve to his solidly muscled legs, their hard lines outlined by his pants. She watched as he walked away, following the slight motion of his firm rear under his jacket.

She'd almost forgotten Aunt Joyce was there when the woman said, "Good for you, dear."

Ruth turned to her in shock. "Um, excuse me?"

"I was simply making the point," she said, "that men don't have a patent on looking. I'm glad to see you're a lady who asserts herself not only in her professional ventures, but . . . beyond."

"Thank you," Ruth said, not at all sure she was hearing correctly.

Aunt Joyce nodded and smiled at her. She tried bravely to smile back. Unable to think of anything else to do or say after that, she picked up her now very diluted Tab.

"Tell me," Aunt Joyce said, "how did you and Frank meet?"

Ruth choked on her Tab. Aunt Joyce waited calmly for her coughing to subside.

"I'm sorry," Ruth whispered finally.

"Not at all. People cough. I'm surprised a health-conscious young woman would be willing to drink that bilge, anyway. You shouldn't have let Frank strong-arm you into it. *I* wouldn't have minded a bit if you'd had the martini."

Ruth began to cough again. Aunt Joyce handed her a glass of water and she sipped it.

"Sorry if I threw you, dear," she said.

"Well," Ruth said, "I am a little . . . um . . ."

"No doubt." The woman leaned closer. Her dark eyes were amused. "You see," she said, "I'm not quite the reactionary old dragon Frank thinks I am. Oh, I have my values; it's just that I'm a bit more . . . *modern* than Frank thinks. Not that it's the poor man's fault." She smiled. "I give him every reason to believe I am the way he sees me."

She craned her long neck to make sure Frank wasn't on his way back yet. "Frank is a wonderful man, but he's stubborn and arrogant. His way is his way and that's that. He was bullheaded even as a boy. Well, he was afraid of his Aunt Joyce then . . . and he's still a little afraid of me. I make sure of it." She smiled again, wickedly. "It does a man like that a world of good to fear *something*. Don't you agree?"

"Yes," Ruth said fervently.

"I don't suppose," the old woman said, "you were surprised to hear me characterize Frank as I did."

"No, actually, I wasn't," Ruth said. She was having a hard time keeping up with the new Aunt Joyce. "I've learned . . . I mean . . . well, we've been at odds." She stopped, not sure how much she wanted to explain.

Aunt Joyce nodded knowingly. "I read the papers," she said. "And, as you see, I know my nephew. I think I have a fair idea what you've been at odds about. If you'll permit me a word of advice . . ."

"Oh, of course," Ruth said, wondering what on earth she was going to hear next. "Please."

"Keep it up," she said. "He's too heavy, and so are the other officers. Don't drop your campaign."

"Thank you." Ruth smiled widely. "Thank you very much."

She saw Aunt Joyce's expression change, and she glanced up to find Frank taking his seat again. When she looked back at the woman, her cool, imperious smile was so unmistakably in place, she had to wonder if their conversation had been a hallucination.

She was still wondering an hour later as she tied her hair back and began to wash her face. In fact, what she'd come to think of as the "other" Aunt Joyce now seemed more a figment of her poor overworked imagination than ever.

There was a knock on her door. "Just a second!" she called. Good; she couldn't wait to tell Joan about the evening. She'd howl when she heard about Aunt Joyce and her now-you-see-it-now-you-don't personality. Maybe Joan had some Devil Dogs. Those would be great right now. Her fish dinner had been nice and virtuous, but she was hungry again.

She rinsed her face, grabbed a towel, and dried off as she went to the door. She opened it.

It wasn't Joan. It was Frank.

She stared at him.

"Hi," he said.

She yanked the ribbon out of her hair and resisted the urge to crawl under the carpet. This made about the trillionth time he'd seen her at her bottom-line worst—wet, makeup-less, wearing some shapeless nothing.

"Hi," she said. "I thought you were Joan."

"Oh?" he said, coming in. "Are you expecting her?"

"No, but she sometimes drops in late on weekends. She brings me Devil Dogs. Listen, give me a minute, okay?" She darted into the bedroom and closed the door.

Her heart was going like a drum. There was something very unsettling about Frank being in her apartment. After all, he hadn't been here for some time now.

"Devil Dogs?" he said from the other side of the door. "Those chocolate things?"

"Yes," she said, hopping as she pulled on just-washed jeans.

"You eat those?"

"I love them."

"Well, well."

"My weakness," she said. She combed her hair madly with her fingers and checked her dresser mirror. It was a mess. She grabbed her brush.

She heard Peaches greeting Frank noisily. He must have picked her up, because the meowing stopped. She brushed some pink blush onto her cheeks, put on lip gloss with her finger, and went out.

Frank was sitting on the love seat in the foyer with Peaches on his lap. As before, the cat was stretched out on her back shamelessly, eyes closed, while he stroked her belly.

"She missed me," Frank said.

"So I see," Ruth said. "You really have the touch. She's usually very shy."

Frank looked up. "You changed. Great. I need some activity after that meal, so I came to see if you wanted to take a walk."

Ruth felt a ridiculous stab of disappointment, but she said, "Sure. I'll get my jacket."

135

Frank gently put Peaches on the floor. She meowed mournfully as they left.

At the outside security door Frank said, "Lock this. It was open when I came in."

"It usually is," Ruth said. "Some of the residents forget to lock it."

"Probably the kids," he muttered as they started down Crestview. "Well, make them cut that out. Lean on them. It isn't safe."

Always quick to blame the kids, Ruth wanted to say, but kept her mouth shut.

They went through Geary Street and came out on the lake track. Frank had put on jeans and sneakers and he was wearing his leather jacket. He didn't take her hand or touch her, but it felt good to have him next to her. His big body radiated a reassuring warmth.

"So," he said as they walked along the track, "what did you think of Aunt Joyce?"

"Oh, she's a riot," Ruth said without thinking.

"A riot? What do you mean?"

"Nothing. I—it was a dumb word. I just meant that I enjoyed meeting her."

"She enjoyed meeting you," Frank said. "She wanted me to be sure and tell you."

"Well, that's very nice."

"Did your nervousness go away fast?" he asked.

"Yes," Ruth said. "Even without a martini."

"Oh." He looked away. "Sorry about that. Aunt Joyce is extremely traditional."

"Mm-hmm," Ruth said.

They walked on without talking. It was chilly but not really cold, and the wind was gentle. There was a tiny sliver of moon, just enough to illuminate the track and rippling patches of the lake. Good thing; Ruth hadn't thought to bring her flashlight. But considering her state of mind, it was fortunate that she'd thought to put on her shoes.

"It's a great night to walk," she said after a time. "How far do you want to go?"

She meant the question innocently, but as soon as it was out in the air something electric happened. The words hung there, echoing.

Frank stopped and gripped her shoulder. "Look, Ruth," he said, "I wasn't craving exercise. I used that excuse so I could be with you."

"You did?" she said stupidly.

"Hell, yes. When have you ever known me to want to exercise?"

He let go of her shoulder and she wished he hadn't —but then his hands were on her face, and he was kissing her, his lips cool, his tongue warm.

"Ruth," he said, dropping his hands to her waist to hold her to him. "I said a lot of things about what was and wasn't going to happen. Well, forget them. I've kept my hands off you long enough. Too long. I'm not going to anymore. I want you like hell."

There was just enough light for her to see his eyes. They held hers fast, daring her to argue but warning her all the same that it wouldn't matter.

She wasn't going to. She would have agreed to be with him no matter what he said he'd come over for, and she wouldn't resist him now. Not a shred of her wanted to do anything but stay in his arms, kiss him more, touch him and be touched. It was time.

"It won't be like before," he said. "That I promise. I've thought about that time so much—wishing it had been different, feeling rotten, feeling . . . a lot of things. Now . . . now I just love you."

"Frank," she said. It came out on a sigh. "I love you too."

With a deep sound of yearning he bent to her mouth again. His hands moved over her back, down the slope of her hips to her thighs.

Everywhere he touched brought tingles of heat. She reached up and wrapped her arms around him and pressed herself closer.

At last, she thought.

She put her hands in his hair and clutched its heavy thickness. For all these weeks she'd only been able to look at him, and she'd looked so long and thoroughly that now that the barriers were down, she didn't know where to touch first, there was so much of him she wanted to learn this way. She moved her fingers to his face and cupped her hands around his hard jawline. She felt the molded lines of bone and the cleft of his chin.

"The last time," Frank said into her hair, "I hated myself. I knew I was too rough with you, and I couldn't stop. Hell, I knew I shouldn't have been there at *all.*"

He stepped back and looked at her. His hands massaged her shoulders, enveloping them. "When I left that day, I swore I'd do everything in my power to forget I'd taken you to bed . . . to forget *you.*"

"And?" Ruth said. "What happened?"

He shook his head. "No go. For a while I had myself convinced that I could see you, work with you, and keep it platonic—but it didn't take me long to realize how full of bull I was. Soon I couldn't stop thinking about you long enough to remember a phone number.

"I was determined to keep my distance as long as I

then they were truly together. "I've wanted this so much."

So different, she thought, so wonderful this time. The motion was a loving force, Frank's body a powerful instrument giving her joy. With every unbearably sweet second, he was bringing them closer, locking them in a bond.

He rolled onto his side and brought her with him. His firm hands on her back kept them one.

"I'm not . . . God, you feel wonderful," he said. "I'm not hurting you?"

"No," she said. "Anything but."

He began to move faster, holding her with him. He took her leg and pulled it over both of his, and she gasped at how it was now, the depth. A second later she began to feel a wash of delight so intense, she didn't want it ever to be over.

His breathing was deafening in her ear as their bodies brought them racing to the ultimate. Ruth lost all awareness and held on to Frank with a grip so fevered and a cry so sweet it sent him spinning into his peak. Ruth was with him, her moan of happiness echoing across the dark water.

CHAPTER EIGHT

"Rats," Ruth said. "I was looking forward to swimming with you."

"I know, babe. I wanted to go too. But this flu thing is turning into a damn plague. With three guys out, I have to be around tonight."

"I understand," she said reluctantly. She gave Peaches a little shove to stop her from chewing on the telephone cord.

"You probably think this is pretty convenient. Things get busy just when I'm supposed to go to the fitness center with you for the first time."

"Well," Ruth said, smiling, "I don't expect miracles. At least you're willing to exercise—even if I practically have to put a spell on you to get you to do it."

"Not always. Give me some credit," Frank said. "*I* asked *you* to go for a walk a few weeks ago. Of course," he said, his voice dropping to a husky whisper, "we didn't walk for long."

Ruth's pulse fluttered as she remembered.

"Ruth?"

"I'm here."

"Were you thinking about that night?"

"Yes," she said.

"I love you, babe."

"I love you too, Frank."

"That's how you know I'm not making excuses," he said. "If we can start out to exercise fully clothed and end up like we did, the possibilities in bathing suits are real interesting. Anyway, maybe we can get together tomorrow night. I'll call you."

Disappointed, Ruth thought about what to do. It was boring swimming laps by herself, but she'd already had a walk today and didn't feel like another one.

Well . . . she'd have loved to play with Frank in the water, but if she couldn't do that, at least it would be refreshing to splash around awhile. She went out, got into her car, and drove to the center.

She found people there she knew, and had a surprisingly good time. She swam, chatted, used the tanning lamp, and ate a frozen yogurt sundae. It was a little after eleven when she went out to her car.

She might have been preoccupied because she was looking forward to seeing Frank tomorrow night—or maybe it was the fact that her jacket hood was up to cover her wet hair, cutting off her hearing a little. Whatever the reason, Ruth wasn't alert enough to know there was a man behind her until his forearm was across her neck, pressing her windpipe.

He had her shoulder-strap purse and her duffel bag before she could even gasp. Without a word, the man let go of her and ran. As he did, she got a look at him. He was more of a kid than a man; he was tall, but he looked about fifteen.

Infuriated, ignoring the sensible instinct that told her to think before she did anything, Ruth took off after him.

"Stop!" she screamed. "Give me my bags back. *Stop!*"

The boy turned to look as he ran. He was at the end of the parking lot, and there was enough light for Ruth to see his surprised expression. But he didn't stop.

"You'd better drop those!" she yelled. "I'm going to catch you! Do you hear me?"

He left the lot and ran down the road, the bags flopping against him. Ruth followed, her sneakers slamming the pavement. She was enraged at losing her things; she couldn't stop screaming. But she was catching up.

"Stop! Drop my bags!" she shouted.

In the back of her mind she knew she was doing the wrong thing. She shouldn't be chasing the kid, and she especially shouldn't be chasing him along a deserted pitch-dark road that was only going to get lonelier and darker. She had to be out of her mind. But she was flat-out damned if she'd give up her good bags and all the things in them without a battle.

Frustrated, she screamed louder.

"You thief! You little criminal! Give those back!"

Just then, the mugger came to a screeching halt. Almost at the same moment as he, Ruth realized that the road had suddenly dead-ended. He looked confused and flustered, then with an awkward movement turned and started running back in Ruth's direction.

Shocked herself, she recovered fast enough to leap at him, but he darted away. Off balance with her target gone, Ruth landed on her belly, skinning her hands and knees on the road. She yowled and jumped up again. The boy was running back toward the center. Ignoring the painful friction of her scraped knees against her pants, she went after him once more.

She knew she should keep quiet to save her wind, but she was too angry. Her bags taken, her knees bloody, her pants torn—it was maddening.

"I'm going to catch you!" she yelled. "Drop my bags, damn you!"

They were back at the parking lot. She was only about twenty feet from the boy now. He looked behind him and saw how close she was.

"Take 'em!" the boy yelled, and threw down the bags.

Ruth grabbed them from the ground. Her breathing was ragged and her heart was thudding, but she was far from worn out.

She looked up. The boy was really flying now without his burden.

The rotten little thief. Where did he get his nerve?

Holding on to the bags, she ran after him again.

He heard her behind him and turned. His eyes went wide. "Lady!" he said, puffing. "You're crazy!"

"*I'm* crazy?" Ruth yelled.

Suddenly he seemed to realize that there was a cluster of people by the entrance of the center. He slowed down to turn once more and she flew at him, hitting him with her duffel bag.

"Stop!" he yelled. "Cut it out, lady!" He tried to protect himself, covering his head with his arms.

Ruth banged herself in the face as the bag rebounded back at her from the force of her blows, but she barely noticed.

"My things!" she screamed. "How dare you take my things!"

"I gave them back!" he shouted. He was darting around the little knot of people, trying to get behind them. His blond hair stuck to his damp forehead. "You got your bags! For God's sake, lady, that's what you're hitting me with! *Stop!*"

"We called the police," a man said.

"Break it up!" another shouted.

Somebody grabbed the bag from her, and Ruth felt her arms being held behind her. She heard a siren.

"All *right,*" the mugger said.

"I'd better not even look at that kid," Frank said, his big fingers probing the bone around Ruth's eye as she sat on the stretcher. "If I get near him, they'll be handing him his teeth. Does it hurt here?"

"No," she said.

"Here?"

"Ouch. A little."

A thin, balding doctor pushed aside the emergency room curtain and came in. "Let me see that," he said, leaning in front of Frank.

"Hold on," Frank said. He lifted Ruth's hair to look in her ears. He tilted her head back to see her nose.

"I'll examine her," the doctor said.

"Just *wait* a minute," Frank said.

"Look, officer—"

"Chief. Relax, will you?" He turned Ruth's hands palm up and squinted at the dried blood. "You must have fought the creep good and hard."

"You bet your badge I did. But that happened when I—"

"This needs to be X-rayed," Frank told the doctor, pointing to the swollen, bruised area below Ruth's eye. "How did he hit you?" he asked Ruth. "Closed fist?"

"He—"

"Do you *mind?*" the doctor said. "I'll make my own

146

examination." He tried to push Frank out of the way. Frank didn't move an inch.

Giving up, the doctor asked Ruth, "Is this the only place you were hit?"

"Yes," Ruth said. "But—"

"I'll pulverize the little crudbucket," Frank said. "I've got him on attempted robbery, I've got him on assault, and I swear, if he broke anything—"

"If he did," the doctor said, "we're not going to *know* about it unless you get out of my way and let me examine the patient."

Frank folded his arms. His dark eyes narrowed. "Look, this isn't just a patient," he said. "That cockroach in my jail picked the wrong woman to take a swing at. This happens to be the lady I love. I—"

"He didn't hit me!" Ruth shouted.

Frank and the doctor looked at her.

"What do you mean, he didn't hit you?" Frank said. He touched her bruise. "Is this from a *kick*? So help me, I'll—"

"It's from my duffel bag. I hit myself with it. I was swinging it at the mugger, and it got me in the eye."

Frank stepped back. The doctor asked him, "Okay if I take my turn now? I wouldn't want to get in your way."

"What about your hands?" Frank asked. He lifted one and gently traced the dark scrapes. "What was he doing to you when you got this?"

"He was trying to get away from me. I jumped at him and missed," she said, holding out her leg so the doctor could roll her pants up. "That's how my knees got cut, too."

"Let me get this straight," Frank said. He leaned against the wall and put his hands in his pockets. "You were carrying two bags, right? The duffel bag and your purse. So he only took the purse? And you defended yourself with the duffel bag?"

"No," Ruth said. The doctor was feeling around her kneecap. "Ouch. He took both bags. I was furious. I ran after him. Later he dropped them, and I picked them up. My face didn't get hurt until the end, just before the police car came."

"You ran after him," Frank repeated with disgust.

"I got my things back, didn't I?"

"Yeah, and you also got this," he said, pointing at her bruise, "and you could have gotten a lot worse! What was he doing to you when you swung the bag at him?"

"Nothing," Ruth said.

"Nothing?"

"Not really. Running around, kind of, trying to get in back of the people who'd come out of the center."

"I don't get it. What for?"

"I think," the doctor said from where he knelt on the floor cleaning Ruth's knee, "the lady you love is trying to tell you she attacked her mugger."

Frank gaped at her. "Is that true?"

"Yes, Frank!" she said. "I was mad!"

"And you already had both bags back?"

"That's right."

He shook his head. He took a pad and pen from his jacket. "This is a damn circus. We're going to start at the beginning."

Ruth said, "The policeman who brought me here already wrote everything down. I don't want to go over it again."

"You have to," Frank said. "I need the details."

"*No.* I'm tired."

148

The doctor stood up. "If you're not going to do what she wants," he said, "I'm getting out of here."

The phone rang. Ruth hurriedly washed the toothpaste out of her mouth, wincing when the motion made her bruise hurt, and ran to answer it.

"Ruth," Frank said, "this kid is just a baby."

"You mean the mugger?" Ruth said.

"Right. I come in here this morning expecting to find a musclebound greaseball with a skull-and-crossbones on his jacket, and there's just a scared little boy huddled in a cell eating Rice Krispies. I released him to his mother."

"You *what?*" she said, feeling sick.

"I had to," Frank said. "He's a juvenile. He wouldn't have spent the night here, except that they couldn't reach a parent, and the juvenile facility in Laconia was full."

Ruth looked at the thick scabby patches on her hands and legs. "Somehow," she said, "he doesn't seem quite like a babe in arms to me."

"I promise you, he's no criminal. He's never done anything before."

"Maybe not—but Frank, what he did, he did to me! I could have lost my things. And I'm all banged up. I never thought this could happen to me. He should be punished."

"Listen. He—"

"And did you say he'll be treated as a juvenile?" she asked. "That just means a slap on the wrist!"

"Ruth," Frank said, a touch of sarcasm in his voice. "Aren't you the one who's always been down on us big bad policemen for torturing 'innocent teenagers'— excuse me, 'children'—for no good reason?"

"Frank, be serious." She got up and began to pace the bedroom. "We're talking about a real delinquent."

Frank sighed. "He's about as far from that as you can get. Real delinquents have more sense and experience than to run down a dead-end street, then turn back around and return to the scene of the crime."

"That's not necessarily—"

"Of course, he ended up regretting that decision once you got to him. He was petrified. He thought you were going to kill him."

"I was really angry," Ruth said. Her knees were starting to hurt from her rapid pacing. She sat down on her bed. "I still am. I look terrible, and I won't be able to walk or run without pain for a while. Is it so bad to want him to suffer too?"

"No, babe," Frank said patiently. "It's natural. But you have to keep that in perspective and not demand more punishment than he deserves. What? Hold on, Ruth."

She heard muffled voices; Frank's was raised in anger. She couldn't make out many words.

He came back on the line. "I have to go," he said. "The board of trustees sent over a regulation they want to push through at next week's meeting, and we're trying to get it voted down. They want us to be subject to disciplinary action and suspension if we're 'significantly overweight.' What the hell does that mean? Are they talking about sideshow freaks, or what? We have the agility, that's what counts."

Ruth was quiet.

"Anyway," he said, "I have as much hassle as I need right now. Can we agree on this mugging?"

"What exactly do you want me to agree to?" Ruth asked.

150

"I'd like you not to press charges. We'll make him get counseling and keep an eye on him, but not through family court. What do you say? Can we avoid an uproar from the victim that justice hasn't been done?"

His tone sounded light, but Ruth wasn't fooled. He had a lot on his shoulders. Still, she wanted time to think. She gave him a noncommittal answer and hung up.

By Sunday afternoon Ruth felt much better. The swelling was gone, and with makeup on the bruise she looked like her old self. There was still some stinging in her knees and hands, but she'd gone for a run and it hadn't been bad.

She still didn't feel as charitable as Frank did about the boy who'd mugged her. Maybe he'd never done it before—but he'd done it Friday night.

And when you're the one it's been done to, she thought as she washed the pan from her grilled cheese sandwich, you want the person to pay.

It was strange how she'd turned around on that. She knew so many terrific kids, and her opinions on teenage crime had always been colored by her respect for them. But having a personal stake in something made a powerful difference.

She supposed that was true about the weight issue, too. She was on the sidelines; Frank was the one directly affected.

She wrung out the sponge and wiped the kitchen table. Regardless, the weight thing was very different. She knew all about the importance of fitness to health —and certainly to a physically demanding job. While she sympathized with the strain Frank was under, she

151

believed more strongly than ever that he needed to shape up his department. He was looking good himself, but he hadn't done much about the others.

Her love for him only increased her concern. She wanted her man protected. His job was dangerous; she learned more about that all the time. And the better condition he and his men were in, the safer he was.

It bothered her that she hadn't been able to change his mind much. He still didn't think anything was needed beyond some occasional lip service. And she hadn't liked it when he told her about the proposed regulation as if he assumed that now that she was in love with him, she'd forget her silly crusade and agree with whatever he thought.

Well, maybe that was unfair. In any case, he *was* right about one thing: she could compromise on the mugging. Being a victim had prejudiced her some. She wasn't as thirsty for revenge today. And since Frank obviously felt strongly about how he wanted to deal with the boy, she would give him her support.

She reached for the phone, but pulled her hand back. It was such a lovely spring day; she'd take a ride over to see him.

She went to his building, but he wasn't home. Could he be working, on Sunday? She drove into town; his car was in the station lot. She parked next to it and debated whether to just go in, or to call from Carolyn's.

She still hadn't been inside the station since the *Banner* article in February. She guessed from things Frank said that no one would give her a hard time, at least not overtly; their relationship was common knowledge, if an object of curiosity.

152

What the hell. She had to go in sometime.

She pushed open the heavy wooden front door. She stood on tiptoe to see through the high window into where the desk man sat—and there was Frank.

He grinned. "Hi, babe," he said. "I just tried to call you a few minutes ago. I left a kiss on your machine. Now I can make good on it."

He got up from the console, went through a door behind him, and came out to lead her inside. Out of sight of the door, he held her chin as if it were a precious gem and kissed her. He examined her eye.

"Looks much better," he said.

"It feels better," she said. "I feel better all over."

He ran a hand down her side, over her waist, and along her firm thigh. "You feel terrific," he said. "If I weren't so busy . . ."

"How come you're here on Sunday?" Ruth asked.

"Damn flu," he said, sitting down and pulling her into a chair next to his. "Everybody's got it. I have two men out in cars, which is the bare minimum, and I had no one to work the desk. So I came in. It was busy this morning, but things are quieter now."

The phone rang. "Lakeboro Police Department," he said. "Chief Gordon." He listened for a minute. "All right, ma'am. Glad you've got him. Thanks for letting us know."

"Lost dog," he told Ruth. "Now a found dog. I like happy endings." He stroked her hair. "It's nice that you came."

"I had a reason," she said.

"You don't need one." He glanced at the door and bent to kiss her neck.

"It's about the boy who mugged me. I was still too

153

upset yesterday to decide, but I won't pursue it. That's what I came to tell you."

"Well, good," Frank said. "You're doing the right thing. Some people would keep gunning for him out of plain vindictiveness—just mad at the world."

The phone rang.

"Lakeboro Police Department. Chief Gordon." He rubbed his forehead. "Yes, I know, ma'am." He listened. Ruth could hear a screechy voice on the other end; it sounded agitated. "We are working on it, that I can tell you. When should you call back? Uh, Thursday. Right. I'm sure we'll have them caught by then. Take care, now."

He leaned back in his chair. "Pygmies," he said.

"Pardon?" Ruth asked.

"That was Mrs. DeRoy. She's being persecuted by pygmies. They climb up on her roof and throw tiles down. They pull up her flowers. They sneak into her house and steal food."

"Good grief," Ruth said. "Is she really dotty, though? Maybe a bunch of kids have her going. Has she ever seen them?"

"Yes," Frank said. "They're orange. Some are green. Some are *striped*. They have thirteen fingers on each hand. They—"

"Never mind. I get the idea."

He put his hand on her neck and pulled her face to his. His kiss was long and warm.

Breathlessly Ruth said, "Should we be doing this here?"

"No," Frank said, standing. "Come with me."

"Where?" she asked, her lips still moist.

"It's a secret."

She looked doubtfully at the array of lights and buttons on the long console.

"It can survive without me for a minute," he said. He led her through the squad room, past the jail with its two empty cells, to a small room with a desk and a bunk bed in it. Judy, the dog, was curled up on the bottom.

Frank pulled Ruth down to sit with him in the space left. He kissed her and undid two buttons of her blouse before she could say a word. He put his hand inside and caressed her breasts where they rose over her bra.

Just that slight touch was enough to make Ruth's heart begin to hammer away, but she said, "What if someone comes in?"

"No one will," Frank said. "If someone was going to, I wouldn't be here. I'd be over at the lake doing this to you. With the smell of spring flowers around us."

"Are you sure?" she asked, her voice softening to a sigh as his fingers went lower.

"Yes, babe." He bent to her mouth. "You're safe with me. You always are. Remember that."

She smiled, warmed by the words. She put her arms around his back and ran them up and down. She loved his bigness, the way she could barely reach around him.

Frank pushed her blouse off her shoulder. His lips followed the ridge of her collarbone to where it ended in the smooth mound of her shoulder, and he kissed her there, letting his teeth lightly scrape her skin.

Ruth felt a warm pressure by her other shoulder. A moment later she realized that what she felt was furry. She turned. Judy had edged her way over and was now occupying half the bunk.

"Frank," Ruth said, and he looked up.

"Damn," he said. "This is her bed. She thinks it is, anyway. Come on."

He grabbed Ruth around the waist and lifted her to the top bunk. He climbed up beside her and drew her down onto the thin mattress.

"You feel so good, babe," he whispered, fitting her against him. He caressed the long line of her thigh under her skirt. "So good."

His hands were turning her into a pool of feeling. Her flesh leaped to vibrant life everywhere they touched. She urged his head down to where her blouse was open, and he kissed the fragrant skin between her breasts. He opened the blouse all the way and she lifted up so he could reach around and open her bra.

The phone rang.

Frank cursed and climbed down. "Don't go away," he said. He grabbed her hand and kissed it. He hurried out to the desk.

Ruth heard him answer. Then, "I'm sorry to hear that, Mrs. DeRoy. Well, no, I'm shorthanded today, but . . . They are? Okay, here's what you do. Tell them Chief Gordon says it's illegal to go up on the roof on Sunday. That's the Sunday Roof Law. Say it good and loud . . . They don't? Well . . . oh, good idea. Yes, I'm sure it'll work. Bye now."

"The pygmies are on the roof?" Ruth asked when he came back.

"Right. And she can't tell them to get down because they don't have ears. So she's going to hang a sign out the window."

"That's nice," Ruth said. He pushed her blouse off her shoulders and opened her bra. "Mmm," she said when his hands covered her breasts. She began to breathe faster. His touch, the caress of his breath on her face as he bent to kiss her, were making her quake. "What if it doesn't work?" she whispered.

He took off her skirt and opened his belt. "Then I'll think of something else. But," he said, getting out of his pants as quickly as possible in the tiny area of the top bunk, "at least it'll take her a while to make that sign. A while I intend to make full use of."

Ruth felt the brush of his hair on her stomach and then the blinding excitement of his mouth. Within moments she'd forgotten where she was, who she was, what year it was. Frank's intimate kiss was magic.

He moved up and took her in his arms. The rough feel of his shirt was unwelcome; she wanted his bare chest against her. She reached for the buttons. He sat up to take it off, and banged his head on the ceiling.

Judy leaped off the bed, barking.

"Quiet!" he said.

Ruth started to laugh softly. Frank grinned, but he wasn't going to be distracted, and hushed her laughter with a deep, loving kiss.

Gently he pushed her legs apart and stroked her satiny inner thighs. The tickle of pleasure was so intense that Ruth couldn't stay still, and when she wriggled, her knee knocked Frank off balance and he started to slip off the bunk.

"Hey!" he said, grabbing the bedpost to steady himself.

Judy began to bark again, loudly.

"Hellfire," he said. "Don't move an inch." He climbed down, took Judy's collar, and walked her quickly out of the room. He shut the door tight and climbed back up.

Immediately Ruth felt his hands again, his lovely hands . . . and then his whole body as he finally brought them together. His breathing went fierce in her ear.

"Ruth," he said, "I love you so much. I could make love to you for the rest of my life."

There was nothing she wanted more. His body driving against hers as he loved her was all there was, everything. Mindlessly she moved with him, faster every second. She felt his mouth on her face, his teeth nipping her ear, now harder as he moved faster still.

A great wave of delight rose up and engulfed her. She heard Frank moan by her ear, and the sound grew louder as he gripped her tight.

Then the wave was so high it blocked out everything. There was no reality but Ruth and Frank and the explosion of joy that consumed them. She hung on to him with her hands, her legs, as they raced together along the top of the wave . . . and then gently, sweetly, down.

"The rest of my life," Frank whispered.

The phone rang.

CHAPTER NINE

Ruth collected the pulse cards and put them in her duffel bag. She looked at the clock. There was a little time before she had to meet Joan for lunch; she could get some errands out of the way.

She heard someone say her name and she turned. A dark-haired man about thirty stood in the doorway of the big aerobics room. He was holding a newspaper and a notebook.

"I'm John Bennett. I'm a reporter for the *Banner*," he said. "Maybe you remember me. I interviewed you in February, after a race."

"I remember you," Ruth said. How could she not? She'd had no inkling then that her brief conversation with him would have such an impact on her life—but she'd certainly thought back on it a lot.

"How can I help you?" she asked. She wiped her forehead. "Are you writing about the fitness center?"

"No," he said. "I'd like to get your opinion on the mugging yesterday."

"Oh, God. There was another one? What happened?"

The man unfolded his newspaper and handed it to her. He pointed to a headline that read, MUGGING VICTIM HURT; OFFICER BLAMED.

"Oh, no," she moaned. She'd thought he wanted her opinion because she was the most recent victim. But she didn't have to read far to know that wasn't why he was here.

A seventy-eight-year-old man had been cornered in an alley two blocks from the town center by a teenager demanding his wallet. It was six o'clock and still daylight. Phil Davids, coming out of Carolyn's, had realized something was happening and started running over to the two men.

Seeing help on the way, the old man had refused to give up his wallet; the boy had gotten more insistent, and had hit the man.

"Police. Hold it!" Phil Davids had yelled at the top of his lungs as he ran to reach them. The boy had turned at that, but seeing that the policeman was still a good distance away, he'd given the old man one more punch before taking off.

The article pointed out that the officer weighed two-fifteen, forty-five pounds over the one-seventy average for his height. It included a quote from Frank, which the *Banner* had run two weeks before in an article about the proposed weight regulation, to the effect that an officer's weight was irrelevant, that all his men were as agile as they needed to be.

Ruth kept her eyes on the paper long after she'd finished reading. They had him; there was no way Frank could stand on that statement now, not when Phil's slowness had so obviously prevented him from protecting the old man. He'd have to admit he'd been wrong.

The reporter clearly expected her to say that. It was how she felt. But why run along with the lynch mob? Speaking out wouldn't achieve anything that wasn't going to happen anyway; the regulation vote had been postponed, but Frank would never be able to keep it down now.

There was plenty of ammunition against Frank. And everybody, Frank included, knew perfectly well what her opinion was. She loved him; she felt committed to him. She couldn't see any good reason to add to the criticism.

She raised her eyes and murmured, "No comment."

" 'No comment'?"

Frank threw the *Banner* down on the floor by Ruth's living room couch. "How much thought did you put in before you said that? About two seconds' worth?"

"It so happens," Ruth said, her voice shaky, "that I thought very carefully before I said anything."

"Oh, you did? And how in hell's name did you arrive at 'no comment'?" He pronounced the words as though they were a preposterous joke. "How did you think that was going to look?"

"Stop yelling!" Ruth said. She was still shocked by the way he'd burst in with the paper, and the fact that he'd been shouting from the moment he got here. "I was trying to help you."

Frank stared at her and raked his hand through his hair. "You really mean that," he said.

"Yes! Of course I mean it!" She swallowed and clenched her hands at her sides. She felt horrible. Things had been so lovely and peaceful with Frank lately, she'd forgotten how *unlovely* they could be.

"Ruth, you don't say 'no comment' when you're trying to help somebody. 'No comment' means 'I know the situation smells, but you won't get me to say so.' It isn't what I expect from you."

"Well, what do you expect? Can we sit? I hate being yelled down at."

He sat on the couch but stayed on the edge. "I expect a supportive statement," he said. "And it isn't too late—you can still make one. All you have to do is call this guy Bennett. He'll print anything you have to say."

She sat next to him—not close, but at least they were both sitting down. It didn't feel so much like a battle that way.

"Be reasonable," she said. "What kind of supportive statement can I make?"

"Give me a break, babe! I'm dodging bullets on all sides!"

"I know," she said. "I feel awful about it. But—"

"What have we been doing the last few weeks? The running, the other sports. I've lost weight. You know I've made an effort. Call Bennett and tell him that."

"He isn't a tape recorder, Frank. He won't just absorb what I choose to say and leave it at that. Once I open my mouth, he can use the opportunity to ask me whatever he wants. And then what do I do?"

"You can manage," Frank said, his eyes hard on hers. "Just field his questions as best you can."

She got up and went to the window. Her throat felt rigid with tension. She looked out and saw redheaded Mike shooting baskets, and realized where her heavy sense of déjà vu was coming from.

Months ago, at the stage in their relationship when there had been nothing between them but antagonism and trouble, Frank had tried to push her into making a statement to the paper. She felt today the way she had then, victimized and furious, caught in a tangle of pressures when all she'd done was what was right.

A lot was different now. She and Frank knew each other and loved each other; they had a future together. They'd managed to get this far despite their awful beginning.

The problem was, the issue that had made it awful had never gone away. They'd been too busy falling in love to realize the potential it still held for getting between them. Well, now it had forced its way in—and it had to be dealt with.

"There's nothing I can do," she said.

"Can? Or will?" Frank got up.

"Can," she said. "It's an impossible situation, Frank. Phil is too heavy to run fast, and a poor old man got hurt because of that."

"It was an unfortunate incident," he acknowledged. "But let's not confuse the incident with the issue."

He went to the door. "I'd like you to think some more about this," he said. "That 'no comment' is a blow. You can take the sting off it." She started to protest. "Just *think* about it, Ruth. I'll call you."

He left.

Ruth went back to the couch and sat down heavily, avoiding the spot that would still be warm from Frank. This was the first time he'd left without a kiss or a hug, and she felt hollow.

Again she thought back to February. Now, he was pushing her more politely—but he was pushing just the same. Uncaring about her convictions, focused only on what she could do for him.

She'd been in a terrible position then, too, but at least there'd been no confusion about what she should do.

What a mess!

* * *

"I'm delighted you could come," Aunt Joyce said. "And we have a lovely day for it. Look—not a cloud."

Ruth dutifully looked up.

"I so wanted us to have lunch on the terrace," Joyce said. She poured burgundy into Ruth's glass and then into her own. The sun winked off the windows of the elegant house. "You do like red wine?"

"Yes," Ruth said. She took a sip. "It's delicious."

"Thank you. Always better at home, too. They don't know what room temperature means in restaurants. Rooms here are kept ten degrees warmer than rooms in France."

She passed Ruth a platter of painstakingly arranged cold roast beef and marinated vegetables. "Please help yourself, dear. All right. Enough small talk. What *is* going on with the police department?"

Ruth looked up sharply. *At least I didn't have a coughing fit,* she thought. "Going on? You mean, aside from what the Banner says?"

"Well, from what I read, Frank is more beleaguered than ever, and with good reason. But he doesn't seem to be doing anything constructive about it. Is that an accurate assessment?"

"I think so," Ruth said, sipping some more wine. Its cool tang was nice on her dry throat. She felt constantly tense these days.

"And the newspaper is trying to stick you back in the middle of it all, but you won't let them. Still accurate?"

Ruth laughed without humor. "It is if you ask me. Frank doesn't see it that way."

"Oh?" Joyce said. She was making short work of a piece of beef, but it didn't interfere with her intense

164

concentration on Ruth. "How does he see it? Wait. Let me guess."

She was quiet while she finished what was on her plate. She picked up a strawberry from a glass bowl on the table. Holding it by the stem, she somehow managed to daintily remove the berry and eat it while leaving the green collar intact.

"Frank," she said, "is obviously still married to the notion that those bull elephants with holsters are as able as anyone to catch criminals. He probably believes a policeman should no more be criticized for his size than for his choice of shirt on his day off. This awful thing with the old man he no doubt sees as a fortuitous stroke for his critics, and an unlucky one for him. Nothing more.

"That being the case," she said, selecting another strawberry, "I imagine he can't for the life of him understand why you, the woman who adores him, aren't leading a phalanx of marchers down Main Street in support of his position—never mind stonewalling the *Banner*. How am I doing?"

Ruth sighed. "Very well, unfortunately." The strawberries looked wonderful; she wished she had the appetite to eat some. "To be fair, though, he isn't quite that black-and-white about it. He has been working to get in shape. I think he realizes that fitness has a bearing on performance. He doesn't take it as seriously as he should, but the last mugging . . . even Frank can't deny that the man didn't have to be hurt."

Joyce raised one eyebrow. Ruth had never known anyone who could actually do that. "My dear," she said, "Frank could look straight at a frog and deny that it's green. I love my nephew more than anyone in this world, and he's a fine, compassionate, principled man

165

—but he's as pigheaded as he is huge. Once he forms an opinion, that's the end. Oh, he might pretend; I've seen him waffle if it suits him, if it helps him get his way. But if you ever think you see Frank Gordon changing his mind about something he's fixed on, take another look."

Ruth ran the big sponge over the Toyota's hood a final time. She rinsed off the suds and started on the chrome.

Usually she paid Mike or Chris to wash the car, but she'd felt like tackling it herself. She was doing that a lot lately, finding mindless jobs that took a lot of elbow grease and tired her out. Sometimes it felt good to be tired. Especially when it meant she was too tired to think.

She stood up to take the strain off her knees for a minute, and saw Frank's Lincoln coming along the driveway. She felt happiness and dread at once.

She hadn't talked to Frank since he'd left her apartment four days ago, his only good-bye a few cool words. She'd done nothing about his request that she talk to the *Banner*. Was he here to push her some more, or would this visit be one that would make the cold knot in her stomach go away?

She wasn't putting money on the second guess. Her lunch with Aunt Joyce had served to color in a picture whose outline she already had.

The whole thing made her want to go find a cave and move into it.

Frank parked next to her and got out. She watched his hard legs inside the dark uniform pants. She saw the ripples of muscle under his shirt as he turned to shut the door. His brown hair blew gently in the breeze. He was a little bit tanned; the face she loved to have next to hers was slightly darker.

"Hi," he said. "Washing the car, huh?"

"Yes," she said.

"How are you?"

"All right. And you?"

"Not bad," he said. He took off his sunglasses. "Not good, either, to tell you the truth. They're voting on the weight regulation the day after tomorrow."

Enough small talk, she thought.

"I could use your help," he said. "The regulation isn't that big a deal; we have a lot of regulations. But a vote of no-confidence is exactly what I don't need right now. It'll shove my back that much harder against the wall."

The image of him shoved hard against anything made her shiver briefly. She said, "You still want me to call John Bennett."

"Yes," he said. He felt the car to see if it was dry and propped his foot on the bumper. "A supportive article would do me some good with the trustees. Even if the vote goes against me, it'd help balance it."

Wisely, he stopped talking and just looked at her.

"Frank," she said, "what do you really think about all this?"

He blinked. "You know what I think."

"No," she said, "I don't. Please tell me."

She saw his jaw move as he ground his teeth. He didn't like this a bit.

He said, "You know what I think because people in love know that about each other. We may not always have the same opinions, but when a man and a woman are as close—"

"Oh, please!" she exclaimed. She hadn't meant to

167

be so loud; it was embarrassing, with all the open windows in the building, and Frank looked startled. But she was hearing exactly what she'd hoped she wouldn't.

"That sounds like greeting-card blather," she said. "I'd like to know where you stand on the weight problem. Do you think your men ought to get in shape?"

"How can you ask me that? I run with you, I watch what I eat—"

"That's not what I asked," she said with dogged patience. She wanted this confrontation as much as she wanted to walk on thumbtacks, but she had no choice. She couldn't sidestep it any longer. "Are you going to keep exercising and dieting, and will you make the department do it too? Or were those things just your way of putting on a show for the town, me included?"

"What is this, a trial?" he asked. He took his foot off the car and put his hands on his hips. "I don't like your attitude. All I did was ask for your support, and you're after me like a damn snapping turtle."

"You're not going to answer me, are you?" Ruth said, dropping her sponge into the bucket.

"Listen, Ruth, I've had about enough," he said. He didn't look so tan now; his face was red with anger. "Get the hell off my back."

"I won't, Frank. I can't." She felt miserable; she hated this. But she could no longer pretend that the peaceful truce they'd achieved over the course of their relationship was real, that it was anything more than Ruth not rocking the boat for Frank's sake.

"You say I'm on your back," she went on, "but what you mean is that I'm not letting you pressure me. It isn't a question of support, either. We love each other.

168

That's one thing. You and your department have a problem. That's a separate thing. You can't mix them the way you're trying to! You can't expect me to do a complete turnaround on what I believe just because I love you!"

"I think," he said, glowering, "that I do have the right to expect support from the woman I love. Hell, Ruth, I'd stand by you no matter what—and you should stand by me."

"I want to stand by you, Frank," she said, "and I have, as much as I could. But you have to meet me halfway. A quarter, even. I want to help you. I'd love to make a statement. That's why I'm pressing you about how you really feel. Give me a reason to make one! Convince me—"

Her words were cut off as Frank grabbed her and pulled her mouth to his. It was a hard kiss that hurt, and the demanding pressure brought tears to her eyes.

"That's the reason!" he yelled, releasing her. "You don't need any more reason than that!"

She caught her breath. He'd just confirmed all she was saying. If she could only make him see!

"You won't understand this," she said, her voice low and tight, "but—*that*—is the reason I won't call the *Banner!* It's because of how I feel about you that I won't say in the newspaper that *I think you're all wrong!*"

"I'm wrong? You don't know what you're talking about!" Frank's rage filled the air between them. "Where do you get off making judgments about police matters?"

"Oh, Frank," she said. "We're not talking about police matters. We're talking about plain common sense and human compassion. A man was hurt! You can't

169

dismiss that! He was hurt because you're too stubborn to—"

"He was hurt," Frank shouted, "because he was the victim of a crime! What the hell's the matter with you that this simple fact of life flies right over your head? Every town has criminals. Criminals commit crimes. Crimes hurt people." He punctuated each point by hitting his palm with his fist. "I only want to be left alone to do my job—which is to see that there are fewer criminals to commit fewer crimes, so fewer people get hurt. You," he went on in a quieter but more menacing tone, "are in a position to help me do that. But will you? No! Because you claim you don't have a . . . *reason!*" He spat the word with a mocking flourish.

"Well, I can't think of a *reason,*" he said, yanking open his car door, "to stand around any longer trying to make sense to someone who won't say a few lousy words to help me out when I badly need it. Who won't support the man she *says* she loves!"

"I do love you!" Ruth cried, her voice raw with anguish. "But how much can you love *me* if all you care about is pushing me to do what you want, no matter how I feel?"

But he was driving away before all her words were out.

"Hate to be a pest," John Bennett said, "but that's what they pay me for. The messages I left on your machine didn't do it, so I thought I'd look for you here."

Ruth paused by the door of the center. "I have a class now," she said.

"Three, isn't it? That's what they told me when I

called." He checked his watch. "You have fifteen minutes. A lot can be said in fifteen minutes. Governments can topple in ten." He grinned.

Ruth didn't grin back. "Look," she said, "I had nothing to say to you before and I have nothing now."

"The trustees are voting tomorrow on whether to make policemen subject to disciplinary action for being overweight," he said. "You must have feelings about that."

I have no feelings left at all.

"Come on, Miss Barrett. What happened to the angry crusader who almost bit my pencil off last February?"

She looked away. "I'm . . . I told you, I—"

"You started a ruckus, a good one." Holding a hand above his eyes to shade them, he made her turn back to meet his intent gaze. "You had guts. *I* think you still do."

She didn't miss the emphasis, but she wasn't going to let John Bennett shame her into saying anything she didn't care to say. She had every right not to speak out.

"And the old man, the mugging victim. What about him?" Bennett asked.

"What about him? He's all right now, isn't he?"

"He *could* have been all right to start with," Bennett reminded her softly. "And, no, he isn't."

"His glasses—"

"His glasses were fixed, but he's in for much more oral surgery than they thought." His gaze darkened. "He's just an innocent old man, Miss Barrett."

Ruth took a deep, hard breath and held it. It didn't help. Two tears spilled down her cheeks.

"Get out your notebook," she said.

171

CHAPTER TEN

"Here's your tea, Frank. Sorry about the vote."

"It's just a regulation, Doreen. We have a lot of regulations." He'd told that to so many people today that it was beginning to sound like a recording. The trouble was, every time he heard the words, he flashed back to the first time he'd said them—to Ruth, in the parking lot, three days ago. It made him go tight with fury all over again.

Well, that would fade. He wouldn't have to feel anger toward her anymore, because he wasn't going to feel anything toward her anymore. She'd humiliated him in public for the second and final time. She was history.

"Want anything else?" Doreen asked. "Pie? A burger? Some carbon monoxide?"

"Pie, I guess," he said vaguely.

"Dandelion or raccoon?"

"Hmm?"

"What kind of pie," she asked slowly, "do you want?"

He rubbed his forehead. "Never mind the pie. I'm not hungry."

Doreen rolled her eyes and left.

He took the tea bag out of the mug, pressed it

against the spoon, and put it on the table. Doreen got ticked when he did that, but it was too bad. If she didn't serve saucers, she was going to have to live with tea bags on the table.

He looked out at the street. It was a warm, gray day, muggy and still. People seemed to be affected by it, and were moving slowly and without purpose. Even the pigeons walking around in front of the movie theater looked listless.

He was in a cruddy mood.

He noticed that a few booths down, on top of one of the jukeboxes, there was a folded *Banner*. He'd made it a point not to bring his copy over here with him, but now he stood up and went to get it. Reluctantly, he unfolded it to the lower half of the front page, to read once more the story headlined POLICE AT FAULT IN MUGGING, HEALTH EXPERT SAYS.

It wasn't there. He turned the paper to see the top. It was yesterday's.

He felt a combination of relief and a queer disappointment.

"Hi, Frank," Phil Davids said. "Okay if I sit down?"

"Hi, Phil. Sure."

The officer slid into the booth with difficulty, his stomach pressing against the table.

"Reading that again, huh?" he asked. "Makes you want to spit, doesn't it?"

"This is yesterday's," Frank said.

"You're reading yesterday's paper?"

"That's nothing," Doreen said, clearing the booth behind theirs. "You should have seen what kind of pie he almost ordered."

Phil leaned forward. "Listen, Frank, about the regulation. It's definite now, isn't it?"

173

"Yes," Frank said.

"So what's the deal, exactly? Will you have to suspend me?"

"I won't suspend you."

"But—"

"What can I get you, Phil?" Doreen asked.

"Oh, uh, nothing, thanks," he said. "I'm not hungry."

"It's catching," she muttered, walking away.

"There's no 'have to' about it," Frank said. He drained his mug and leaned back in his seat. He folded his arms. "I'll eat my badge before I'll suspend you or anyone for refusing to diet."

"But I'm not refusing. Debbie's always on my case about how much blubber I've got. This is as good a time as any to start working it off."

"Well, the whole point is that it's up to you," Frank said. His dark eyes were determined. "Your weight is your personal business. I won't have the damn trustees thinking they can regulate something like that. Hell, next thing, there'll be a regulation about what brand of deodorant we have to use."

He looked out the window again. There was Terry Daniels, pulling out of the lot in a squad car. Terry had come to his office with the same sheepish expression Phil wore now, asking the same thing. It made him want to throw plates against the wall. Why should his men have to worry about keeping their jobs for such an idiotic reason? They were fine officers. It was crazy.

"The thing is," Phil said, "it's been on my mind. I keep thinking back on the mugging. Seeing myself running down the street. It seems like it took two hours."

174

"God, Phil, don't do that to yourself. We all wish we could prevent things. You can't dwell on it."

Phil was quiet, and his round face looked unhappy.

"Look at it this way," Frank said. "You prevented a worse injury. Don't kick yourself because of what you didn't do."

"I can't help it. What they're saying is true. I'm way out of shape."

Frank slammed his hand on the table, rattling the mug and spoon. "Cut it out!" he said. "You're a great cop. The best. Stop feeling sorry for yourself. That's an order."

"Would you mind," Doreen called from the counter, "holding the karate championships somewhere else?"

Frank got up from the couch and turned off the TV. Nothing was on that he wanted to watch. He picked up the *Banner*, and then dropped it as if it had burst into flame. He sure as hell didn't want to read *that*. In fact, there was no point in even keeping it. He'd thrown out his office copy; this one deserved the same fate.

He took it into the kitchen and dropped it in the trash. For good measure he poked it down with a paper towel roller in the basket, dumping some eggshells and a couple of dripping cans on top of it.

Now what did he want to do?

He filled the tea kettle and turned on the stove, but immediately turned it off. He'd had enough tea today to float a destroyer. He didn't really want any more.

What he really wanted was to hit the sack. This had been one miserable write-off of a day, and it was just about over. He didn't usually go to bed for another hour or so, but what the hell. Tomorrow was bound to be better, and it would be tomorrow that much sooner if he declared today finished.

Besides, he was wiped out. He hadn't been able to keep his eyes open long enough to finish watching the news.

He got undressed and took a long, steamy shower; it drained what little energy he had left. He climbed into bed and was out in seconds.

He wasn't sure what woke him. The big red numbers of his digital clock-radio said one-twenty. He'd only been asleep for two hours.

He turned his pillow over and closed his eyes.

For a long time nothing happened. He shifted around, trying to get comfortable. He tried two pillows, and then no pillows. Finally he dozed, but he woke again before he was fully asleep.

He got up and went to the kitchen, feeling antsy and frustrated. He started for the stove, and then turned to the refrigerator instead, deciding to have a beer.

He thumbed open the cold can and sat down at the kitchen table. His eyes started to close, and he rested his head in his hand. Damn, he was tired. So why couldn't he sleep? Well, if he was going to be drifting off like this, he was going to get more comfortable. He got up, picked up his beer, and went to the living room couch.

Soon he was weaving in and out of a fitful sleep, and dreaming a strange dream. In it, Phil Davids was running down Main Street, his heavy legs moving in an odd rhythm.

Then he realized that he was looking at Phil through a window—the window of Carolyn's. It distorted the scene slightly. And what was odd about Phil's legs was that they were going in slow motion—even though the cars and the other people on the street were moving normally.

"It seems like it took two hours."

That was funny. How could he be hearing Phil talk when Phil was out there on the street?

He looked where the words had come from. Phil was in the booth with him, his round belly touching the table.

Doreen said something; the voice didn't sound like hers, though, so he turned to look at her. It wasn't Doreen standing by the booth. It was an old man wearing broken glasses.

Frank opened his eyes. He was suddenly thoroughly awake, and very lucid.

It was clear to him now. Slow motion. That was the problem, all right.

It had taken a silly dream to show him, but all the pieces had finally fallen together into a picture even he couldn't ignore—Frank Gordon, Chief of the Lakeboro Police, Captain of Because-I-Said-So.

They were right, all of them: Ruth, Phil, everyone who'd tried—tactfully or not so tactfully—to tell him. He was a great leader, but lately he'd been a great leader with cotton over his eyes. He had to shape the men up, for the good of the town.

Of course the outside door was unlocked. He'd told her a thousand times not to let that happen. Even at eight thirty in the morning on the Saturday before Memorial Day, you never knew what kind of character might be shagging by.

In this case, though, it was lucky for him. He could go right up to her apartment without any nonsense about having to be buzzed in.

177

He went to her door and knocked. There was no answer. He swore. He wanted to see her *now,* say his piece *now.* He felt heartsick over everything that had happened; he didn't want to wait to start making it better.

He knocked a last time, good and loud. Nothing. He started to leave.

He heard noises inside. He put his ear to the door. Yes, definitely.

"Ruth," he said. "Open the door. Please."

She wouldn't answer.

"I have to talk to you. Come on, babe. I promise, you won't be sorry."

Still she didn't say anything. He wracked his brain for convincing words, for something that would show her he knew what an awful fool he'd been. The trouble was, he didn't feel like shouting all that for the whole building to hear.

He knelt down to look for her feet under the door. If she was next to it, she'd hear him even if he talked low. But the crack wasn't big enough to see through.

"Ruth," he said urgently, his head touching the floor. "Ruth! Please answer me."

Nothing.

"Ruth!"

"What on earth . . . ?"

He twisted around, slamming his elbow on the door frame. He rubbed it, wincing. "I'm trying to talk to Ruth," he told Joan, who stood on the stairway looking bewildered.

"She's not home," Joan said.

"Yes, she is, damn it. I can hear her." He put his face to the bottom of the door again. "Ruth, I know you're there. Listen, your neighbor is right here with me. Open up, will you?"

"I'm sure she isn't there," Joan said, coming down the last few stairs. "I saw her run up the street half an hour ago. She won't be back for a while."

"Come here," he said.

Looking more baffled than ever, she walked over to where he knelt.

"No, down here. Listen under the door. Tell me you don't hear her."

Joan gave him a long look, sighed, and got down on her knees. She put her ear to the bottom of the door.

Very clearly they both heard, "Meow."

"Lakeside Fitness Center, good morning."

"Good morning. What time are Ruth Barrett's classes today?"

"Ruth teaches aerobic dancing, sir. We have no coed aerobics classes. May I tell you about our Pumping Iron workout?"

"No, thank you. I only want—"

"If you're interested in aerobic exercise, we have an advanced calisthenics class. We call it the Hollywood Body Shop. Our men clients just love it."

"It's Ruth Barrett that I—"

"I'm sorry, but as I said, Ruth doesn't teach coed sessions. We do have many other fine instructors. Are you familiar with our Neptune Swim? Mr. Nick teaches that. I'm sure he'll—"

"I need to reach Ruth Barrett," Frank said loudly and firmly. "She won a lottery prize. When will she be in?"

"A lottery prize? Well, that *is* exciting. She's off today, but she'll be here Tuesday morning. Why don't you give me your—"

He hung up.

"This is Ruth Barrett. I'm not available right now, but please leave a short message after you hear the tone, and I'll call you back as soon as I can."

Beep.

"Ruth, this is Frank. Listen, babe, I've got to talk to you. I went to your place and called the center, but I couldn't find you. I was wrong. You weren't being unreasonable—I was. We're going to start over once more, and this time it's going to—"

Beep.

"Hello?"

"Ruth, thank God. I've been leaving messages on your machine all day. I— Ruth? *Ruth?*"

She had hung up on him.

Frank parked the Lincoln near the basketball hoop. As he'd hoped, there were several boys on the court. He spotted Chris Lindsay and called him over.

The others stopped playing and watched. He couldn't blame them. Naturally they'd wonder why the police chief had come to talk to Chris. Especially when he was carrying a big box of Devil Dogs.

"Will you do me a favor? An easy one," he said, holding out some money.

Chris looked at the money. "Two dollars? For what?"

"All you have to do," Frank said, "is take this box up to Ruth Barrett. She's home; I just . . . talked to her.

Keep the envelope right on top, and make sure she opens it and reads the note."

"That's all?" the boy asked dubiously.

"That's all. Will you do it?"

"Sure," he said. He put the money in his pocket, took the box, and ran inside. The other boys went back to their game.

Frank waited, tapping his foot on the blacktop of the basketball court. His mouth was dry; he swallowed, but it didn't help. He felt sweat starting at the back of his collar, and he scratched his neck. He kept his eyes on Ruth's windows. He couldn't see inside at all.

Very soon Chris came down the stairs and out the door, still carrying the box.

"Sorry," Chris said. "She told me to give it back. Do you want the two dollars back?"

Frank swallowed again. "No. What did she say?"

"Well, she was real friendly at first. But then when I told her you wanted her to open the envelope, she said, 'I thought these were from your mom. I won't take them.' And she closed the door. Are you sure you don't want the money back?"

"No, Chris. Thanks anyway."

He got back into the car and left.

"Hello?"

"Ruth, don't hang up. You've got to give me—"

"Damn it, Frank. What does it take to get a message through to you? *Stop calling! Leave me alone!*"

"No! Whatever it takes, I'll keep—"

"You think that if you just push hard enough, you can get whatever you want! Well, you can't. You can't get me." She began to sniffle.

"Please don't cry. Everything's going to be different now. I—"

"I don't believe you! I'll never believe you! You'll say anything! I f-fell for that enough. Your nice words don't m-mean anything. *Don't call me again!*"

Then he heard the dial tone in his ear.

It was nearly dark. Ruth went around turning on lights, but that only made the apartment a lot brighter than she felt, so she turned them off again—all but a dim lamp in the living room—and sat on the couch.

Frank had finally stopped calling. She supposed she was glad—as glad as she ever was about anything nowadays. After all, it was what she wanted, she reminded herself.

But the tears in her eyes belied the conviction of her words, and she trembled as she covered her face with her hands.

For the eightieth time he wondered if it would work. If it didn't he was going to feel like a hell of a jerk, setting all this up for nothing. But that wouldn't matter much compared to the bottom line: he'd still be without Ruth.

Ruth-less.

He chuckled humorlessly.

"You say something, Frank?" Terry Daniels asked.

"Nope," he said.

Phil Davids caught up to them. He was breathing hard. "Aren't we . . . supposed to be talking?" he asked.

"Yeah," Frank said. "That's how you know if you're . . . running at the right . . . pace. If you can keep up a . . . conversation."

"Hey, Chief," one of the other men called from behind. "Can we . . . slow it down a little?"

"No," Frank said. "Any slower and we'd . . . be taking a . . . stroll. Get used to it, Hunt. We're going to . . . be doing a lot . . . more of this."

The two *Banner* people in the golf cart caught up with the runners. "I want some shots of all five of you together," the photographer said. "Get closer. Chief, stay in the lead. That's it. Good. And another. Good."

Frank sneaked a look behind him. They were a rag-tag pack all right, a bunch of half-dressed cops with their excess weight jiggling as they ran. Hairy winter-white legs stuck out of long-unused athletic shorts—very large ones, and, in two cases, very outgrown ones. They were all puffing and sweating, but at least they were keeping up.

Frank had more regard for them than he could ever say. He'd assured Phil Davids two days ago at Carolyn's that he was a fine cop, and he meant it. But it had taken that unending, haunting, sleep-starved night for him to realize just how fine Phil really was—and Terry, and Pat Hunt, and the other guys. They'd all grown to see—while their bullheaded chief was still stomping around defending the status quo like it was Iwo Jima—that the critics were right: they were unfit to do their best. Their bodies had grown out of line with their dedication.

That night he'd finally understood why Phil couldn't stop thinking about the injured man. He'd understood because he couldn't stop *dreaming* about him. And what had really come clear, as the hours wore on, was that they were lucky—the department, and especially himself as their leader—that more people hadn't been hurt before they learned.

Now the one big job still left was to convince Ruth, his adored and dearly missed Ruth, that his change in attitude was for real. He'd decided his best chance was to stop yapping and show her—which was why all five of them were out here on the track at this particular moment, timed to coincide with Ruth coming the other way very soon. And to really drive the point home, he was showing all of Lakeboro too; the pictures shot from the golf cart would accompany an interview he'd given to John Bennett.

They'd reached the part of the lake where he was going to find Ruth. The track was more enclosed here, with rocky outcroppings and dense bushes. He took another look behind him. He hoped the guys would *live* long enough to meet her. They were panting hard, and very red in the face.

What a great bunch they were: the chief kept going, so they kept going. He slowed a bit, gradually; his anxiety had been pushing his pace up, and that wasn't fair to them.

They jogged on. Probably just a minute or two more. He was getting more nervous as they got closer to the meeting point. What if . . .

There were too many what-ifs to count.

The path twisted a lot now, winding through the brush. Sunlight winked off the water and flickered through the leaves. It was in his eyes for a minute, and the next minute he ran around a stand of rock, and then there was Ruth, in white shorts and a tank top, five feet from him.

He hadn't considered what her instinctive response might be to suddenly coming upon a wall of big men blocking the track—so he was unprepared for what happened next. Prevented by the rocks from dodging off the path to her right, Ruth jumped to her left. Her foot hit the sloping ground at a poor angle and she stumbled and fell, rolling down the embankment.

Idiotically, Frank thought, Well, at least it's not February, and hustled after her. He wasn't fast enough. They all heard the splash.

When Ruth surfaced she saw a number of hands reaching out to her. Treading water, she stared stupidly at them. She couldn't quite get herself to act.

She heard Frank's voice. "Here! Come here!" he was calling, and she looked up at him. "Take my hand!" he said.

She moved to it. He gripped her arms, then her waist, and hauled her out.

"Ruth," he said. "Ruth." He hugged her dripping body to him.

She looked at the other men. They were flushed and sweaty. They seemed bewildered. A movement caught her eye: a man was clicking away with a camera, darting around them.

"Are you all right?" Frank asked anxiously. His hands explored her tenderly, as if to make sure she wasn't broken.

"Yes, I'm fine, I think," she said blankly. "Just wet."

She wiped water from her face and squeezed it out of her hair. The motion seemed to send her brain back into gear.

"Frank!" she said, scrambling away from him. "I told you—"

"Look!" he said. "Look around!" He had a strange expression on his face, full of pain and desperation. "We were running, all of us. Not just for show—this is real. Look." He pointed to the man with the camera.

She spotted John Bennett behind him. "He's taking pictures for the *Banner*. They'll go with a story John is writing about how the police department is on a *permanent* diet and exercise program." He stared hard at her, his eyes probing, full of hope.

"Oh," she said, understanding at last. "You do mean it."

"Yes."

"You really, *really* mean it!"

"Yes!" he said.

She heard a click and then several more as Frank's arms went around her.

"It wasn't only because I love you," Frank said as they lay on the grassy shore after the others had left. "It was because I also love this town and my job that I finally got it together. I'm not proud of how long it took, but I'm going to make up for lost time."

"Are you . . . talking about the department?" Ruth asked.

He stroked her face, pushing her damp hair back. "I'm not talking about the department at all," he said, looking intently at her. "If you have to be out of my sight long enough to teach a class, I'll live with it, but otherwise I want you with me full time. That okay with you?"

Ruth smiled. In the last two hours, all the things she'd seen and heard had fused together to show her that Frank had genuinely changed, leaving her buoyant and free and more deeply happy than she'd ever been.

"Oh, Frank," she said. "It's very okay with me." She lifted her face, and his mouth covered hers in a kiss of true belonging.

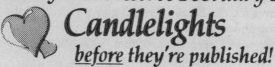